The cheetah saw its chance. In the blink of an eye, the cat became a spotted blur streaking across the plain as it torpedoed towards its victim. This time Jake was ready for the thrust of power when Brandon accelerated. The bike surged forward, its front wheel momentarily leaving the ground before hitting the earth hard again. Jake clung on while managing somehow to keep the cheetah in the viewfinder.

Just seconds into the chase, Brandon yelled out to Jake, 'He's doing nearly a hundred kilometres an hour!'

Sprinting at full speed, the cheetah hardly seemed to touch the ground. It flew across the savannah, reaching so far forward with its hind legs that its back feet hit the ground in front of its head, bending its body almost into a circle. Jake almost forgot to breathe. He'd never experienced anything so exciting in his life!

LUCY DANIELS

SAFARI SUMMER

CHASE

Illustrated by
Pete Smith

Hodder
Children's
Books

a division of Hodder Headline Limited

Special thanks to Andrea Abbott

**Thanks also to everyone at the Born Free Foundation
(www.bornfree.org.uk) for reviewing the
wildlife information in this book**

Text copyright © 2004 Working Partners Limited
Created by Working Partners Limited, London W6 0QT
Illustration copyright © 2004 Pete Smith

First published in Great Britain in 2004
by Hodder Children's Books

The rights of Lucy Daniels and Pete Smith to be identified
as the Author and Illustrator respectively of the Work
have been asserted by them in accordance with the
Copyright, Designs and Patents Act 1988.

For more information about Lucy Daniels,
please visit www.animalark.co.uk

10 9 8 7 6 5 4 3 2 1

A Catalogue record for this book is available from
the British Library

ISBN 0 340 87850 9

Typeset in Palatino by Avon DataSet Ltd,
Bidford-on-Avon, Warwickshire

Printed and bound in Great Britain by
Clays Ltd, St Ives plc

The paper and board used in this paperback by
Hodder Children's Books are natural recyclable products
made from wood grown in sustainable forests.
The manufacturing processes conform to the environmental
regulations of the country of origin.

Hodder Children's Books
a division of Hodder Headline Limited
338 Euston Road
London NW1 3BH

ONE

'Watch out! That one's going to charge!'

The warning shout from Jake Berman's stepdad, Rick, came just in time. In a split second, the mud hole erupted and a huge adult hippopotamus burst out. With clods of mud flying from its thick black hide, the angry hippo stormed straight for Jake and Rick who were at the top of a dusty slope just metres away.

'Into the truck, quick,' ordered Rick, sprinting back to the Land Rover which was parked not far behind them.

Jake dived through the passenger door just as Rick slammed the vehicle into reverse. He clung tightly to the dashboard as Rick swung the vehicle round, its wheels spinning in the dust.

With a speed and agility that left Jake breathless, the hippo crested the slippery bank and hurtled across the rock-hard ground. 'That animal can *move*!' Jake exclaimed, seeing how fast it was gaining on them with every stride of its stubby legs. He braced himself, fully expecting the hippo to catch up with them and ram the side of the Land Rover. But Rick accelerated and quickly outstripped the hippo, so that moments later the bulky creature gave up its bad-tempered chase and came to a sudden halt.

'Phew! That was close,' Jake panted, leaning out of the window and looking back. The hippo stood and glared after them, like an over-sized watchdog that had seen off an intruder.

This wasn't the first time Jake had faced a rampaging wild animal. He'd had a few narrow escapes since coming to live in the Musabi Game Reserve in Tanzania with his mum, Hannah, and new stepdad, Rick, who was the chief warden. A couple of those were from charging elephants, like the time a female called Rosa nearly flattened Jake when she thundered past him to rescue a calf trapped in mud. And before that there had been the lioness trying desperately to reach her cubs through a fence. Jake had been in a hide just yards away, so he'd seen for himself the incredible strength of the frustrated lioness.

All these encounters had taught Jake just how dangerous and unpredictable wild animals could be. Even so, he was completely unprepared for the way the hippo had burst out of the mud and, for no obvious reason, hurtled towards him and Rick.

It was an early November morning and Jake, who was home for a week from boarding school in Dar es

Salaam, had come with Rick to check on the small herd. Like the other hippos in the reserve, these four animals were desperately seeking shelter from the relentless sun in a meagre patch of mud. Normally the hippos would spend all day submerged in deep pools, only coming out onto the land to feed at night. But now, because of the drought that was gripping Tanzania, most of the rivers and water holes had dried up, leaving many of the hippos in Musabi high and dry. If it didn't rain soon, even the mud holes would disappear and then the hippos would be in real trouble.

Jake knew this would leave Rick with no choice but to move the most vulnerable hippos to man-made water holes. There were five of these dotted about in different parts of Musabi. When the drought began to bite hard several weeks ago, Rick and his staff had set about forming the emergency pools. A hired earth-moving machine had dug deep, wide holes and these were then lined with sheets of plastic. Finally, water was pumped in from nearby boreholes which had been sunk in the last drought several years before.

With the water holes ready, Rick was deciding which hippos in the reserve needed to be relocated most urgently. He'd been monitoring this herd for the past week and he and Jake had only just climbed out of the Land Rover for a closer look when the hippo charged.

'I thought you were being too careful when you said we had to stay close to the Land Rover,' Jake confessed to his stepdad. 'I mean, those four hippos were so still they looked fast asleep.'

Rick drove off a short way then pulled up in the sparse shade of a spindly thorn tree a few hundred metres from the mud hole. 'Just proves what I'm always telling you,' he said, turning off the engine. 'You can never be too careful in the bush.'

Metres away, the hippo stared suspiciously at them for a while before whirling round and running back to the mud hole.

'What was all that about?' Jake wondered out loud. 'It's not as if we were doing anything threatening,' he added, thinking that perhaps the drought was making the hippo more aggressive than usual.

Rick leaned forward, his arms resting on top of the steering wheel, and watched the hippopotamus settle into the sludgy ground alongside the calf.

'She thought we were,' he said. 'You see, that little one's her baby.'

'Oh, I get it,' Jake said. 'She was protecting it.'

'Uh-huh,' confirmed Rick. 'And don't think that was just a mock charge to warn us off. Hippos don't bother with niceties. If they go for you, they really mean business. That's what makes them the most dangerous animals in Africa.'

'How do you mean?' Jake was surprised by Rick's comment.

Rick looked at him and said soberly, 'Hippos are responsible for killing more people on this continent than any other creature. Except for malaria-carrying mosquitoes, of course.'

Jake felt astonished. Surely other animals – like lions and buffaloes – were a lot more dangerous? 'And crocs? What about them?'

Rick nodded. 'Oh, sure. Crocs are lethal, especially when they're looking for a meal. But they're nothing like hippos when it comes to aggressive attacks on humans. As you've just seen for yourself, hippos are very protective of their young. Get too near a mother hippo and her calf, or between a hippo and the water, and you're history.' He listed his hands off the steering wheel and clapped them together. The noise echoed sharply in the heat-stifled air of the African bush. 'One snap of those jaws is enough to cut a man in half.'

Jake shuddered. Imagine staring into the cave-like mouth of a furious adult hippo, knowing that at any moment . . . 'Ouch,' he muttered. He picked up a pair of binoculars from the dashboard and trained them on the herd. The four animals lay squashed tightly together in the shallow mud. With their hides fully exposed to the sun and with no way of cooling themselves off until dark, they looked very uncomfortable. Jake could see a series of lurid pink scars criss-crossing their backs, almost like roads on a map. 'It looks like the sun's cracking their hides,' he remarked. 'They can't be happy in that bit of mud. And there's nothing much for them to eat round here.' He looked around at the hard-baked earth. There was hardly a blade of grass in sight, and what little vegetation there was had dried out long ago. 'Maybe we should have brought them some bales of hay.'

'Hunger's not their worst enemy right now,' responded Rick. 'More like dehydration. Hippos are a hundred per cent dependent on water to survive.'

Jake stared at the herd's muddy resting place. It seemed to be drying up before his eyes. A stream of sweat trickled down Jake's forehead. He wiped it off with the back of one hand then looked up at the cloudless sky, squinting against the harsh white glare of the relentless sun. If only it would rain! The last downpour had been months ago. 'I'd say this herd needs to be moved fast,' he observed to Rick.

'Yep,' Rick agreed. 'They're a lot worse off than when I saw them a couple of days ago.'

'So do we move them today?' Jake persisted. He had a good idea of what was involved in moving big animals because he had helped to relocate a herd of ten elephants brought to Musabi from an overcrowded game reserve in Zambia. It had been an awesome experience, involving a helicopter and a large team of helpers as well as a fleet of trucks. With the hippos though, it would be a lot easier.

'Moving them will be a piece of cake compared to the elephants,' Jake reminded Rick. After all, there were only four hippos and they wouldn't be going very far. Also, the game capture truck and equipment were ready back at the main camp. It would just be a matter of driving the truck down to the mud hole, tranquillizing the hippos, then guiding them onto the back of the lorry and driving them to one of the temporary drinking holes.

Rick nodded. 'They shouldn't cause us too much trouble,' he said. 'So the sooner the better.' He started up the engine once more. 'We'll take them to the water hole near the house.'

'Great,' said Jake enthusiastically. 'We'll be able to keep an eye on them there.'

The hour-long journey back to the ranch-style house where the Bermans lived seemed almost endless in the midday heat. With the sun beating down on him through the widescreen, Jake kept thinking of the hippos. *At least I can jump into the swimming pool to cool down*, he told himself when he and Rick finally turned into the driveway and he caught a glimpse of the sparkling pool that was fed by a borehole in the garden.

But Jake's thoughts of a refreshing swim vanished when he saw a green jeep parked under the fig tree on the lawn. What caught his eye most of all was the dirt bike standing on a trailer behind the open-top jeep. Jake looked appreciatively at the big-wheeled motorbike. 'Visitors?' he asked, trying to think which of their friends might own the bike.

Rick shrugged. 'Dunno,' he said, pulling up next to the jeep. He opened his door. 'We weren't expecting anyone today, as far as I know.' He sounded irritated by the thought of having to play host when there was so much to do on the reserve.

It's the drought, Jake thought, jumping down from the Land Rover and following his stepdad towards the house. *Everyone's sick of it – Rick, the hippos. Even me.* He swiped at a fly that was pestering him. It had buzzed around his head all the way from the hippo hole and now it was following him onto the veranda. 'Pest!' he said, just as the screen door leading from the house opened and two familiar figures – a tall dark-haired man and a slim blonde woman – came out.

'Pest! Who? Us?' asked the man with a broad grin.

'Brandon! Sophie!' Jake exclaimed, then quickly added, 'No, a fly's the pest. But, hey! I thought you were arriving later in the week.'

'That was the original plan,' smiled the young woman whose accent was unmistakably American. 'But we'd finished all our business in Dar es Salaam . . .' she glanced at Brandon, 'Or should I say, Brandon found a second-hand dirt bike really fast! So there wasn't much point in hanging around town any more.'

'And we just couldn't wait to get back here,' added Brandon. He shook Rick's hand and gave Jake a friendly slap on his shoulder. 'We called Hannah this morning and she said it would be fine to come straight on down today.' He looked out across the garden towards the wilderness of Musabi. 'It's great to be here again.'

This was the second time Sophie and Brandon Masters had come to Musabi. But they weren't tourists. They worked in the film industry and their first visit had been with an American film company to make a movie set in the game reserve. Brandon, a famous Hollywood actor, was the star of the film along with a pair of lion cubs, while Sophie was the animal trainer. The couple had married soon after returning to America and now they were back in Tanzania to make another film, this time a documentary on cheetahs, the first in a series entitled *Incredible Felines*.

'I'm looking forward to another sprinkling of Musabi magic,' smiled Sophie, linking her arm through Brandon's. 'Our lives certainly changed for the better on our first trip here.'

'You can say that again. I ended up with a wife and a new career,' laughed Brandon who, after working with the lion cubs, had traded in the limelight of being a Hollywood superstar to become a wildlife documentary maker. 'Who knows what might happen this time?'

'Yeah. A hippo might want to run you down like a steam roller,' Jake teased.

Sophie gave them a puzzled look, but before she had time to say anything the screen door swung open again and Jake's mum, Hannah, came out. 'What's this about hippos and steam rollers?' she said, looking anxiously at Jake and Rick.

'We're both OK,' Rick quickly assured her, then outlined what had happened at the mud hole.

'Sounds pretty nerve-wracking,' said Sophie when Rick had finished.

'And it must have been quite something to see,' said Brandon. 'At the risk of sounding, er . . . bloodthirsty, I'm just sorry we weren't there to film it. After all, no one was hurt and it would have made for some unique footage – the kind that would make our documentary stand out from all the others.'

'But aren't you making a film on cheetahs?' said Jake, frowning.

'Yes. And it's going to be amazing: we're going to race one to measure its speed,' answered Brandon, glancing across the lawn to the motorbike. 'Thanks again for giving me permission to do that, Rick,' he said, then turned once more to Jake. 'But apart from shots of cheetahs, we also need background footage of scenery and animals to link the different sections of the documentary.'

'And the hippo chase would have been perfect,' put in Sophie. 'But for more than just background scenes. You see, we're looking for unusual footage.

Rare events perhaps, or animals hardly ever captured on film. Something that could put us in the running for the Heritage prize.'

'What's that?' Jake asked.

'The equivalent of an Oscar, only it's for wildlife documentaries rather than feature films,' Brandon explained.

'You could come with us when we move the herd this afternoon,' suggested Rick.

Hannah looked appalled. 'I hope you're not going to look for trouble.'

'Rick look for trouble?' echoed Jake, who'd never known his stepdad to take even the slightest uncalculated risk in the bush. 'Not in a zillion years!'

'Would you like to have a go with the camera, Jake?' asked Sophie.

It was later that afternoon and they were back at the mud hole. Rick and his right-hand man, Morgan Rafiki, had darted the three adult hippos with a tranquillizing drug. This made them docile so that they could be prodded up a ramp onto the back of the game capture truck. Jake had helped by guiding the calf, which was only about a month or two old, up the ramp behind his mother. The little animal reached almost to Jake's knees and Jake had walked behind him, his hands on either side of the calf's dry, leathery belly, to make sure it didn't fall off the ramp.

Brandon and Sophie had filmed the whole operation,

including Jake ushering the calf along. While Rick and Morgan removed the ramp and secured the back of the truck, Sophie offered the neat hand-held camera to Jake, together with the chance to film the hippos being driven away from their muddy prison.

Jake's eyes lit up. 'You mean it?' he gasped, and when Sophie grinned and nodded, he carefully took the small silver video camera from her. Jake was quite keen on photography, thanks to his mum who was an award-winning wildlife photographer.

Sophie pointed to a couple of buttons. 'That's to record and that's the zoom function,' she said. 'The rest is pretty much automatic.'

'Except for the creative side of filming,' Brandon chipped in. 'Getting the shots that will speak a thousand words, that sort of thing. That's up to the cameraman.'

'I'll do my best,' Jake promised, peering through the colour view finder. He was sitting on the bonnet of Sophie and Brandon's jeep at the top of the same slope the angry mother hippo had stormed up that morning. From this elevated position, Jake had a good view of the four animals that were standing side-by-side behind the strong metal bars enclosing the back of the truck.

He pressed the record button and zoomed in on the hippos, singling out the calf and focussing for a moment on its jowly face. At the same instant, the baby hippo obligingly opened its mouth in a wide yawn. *Perfect*, Jake thought, concentrating on keeping his hand steady. Next, he zoomed out to film the barren landscape before doing a close-up of the muddy spot where the hippos had waited in vain for the rain to come. *One day, you'll be able to come back home*, he silently promised the hippos. *But for now, you're going to a place where you can be safe from the drought.*

Rick and Morgan climbed into the truck and slammed their doors. 'See you all later,' Rick called out of his window before starting up the engine.

Jake switched off the camera and handed it to Brandon, then climbed into the back of the jeep. He was going back to the house with Brandon and Sophie because Brandon wanted to try out his new bike before nightfall. He had invited Jake along which made for a difficult choice – Jake could either see the hippos settling into their new temporary home, or go on the bike. In the end the bike won; riding a dirt bike through Musabi at sunset wasn't something Jake would often get the chance to do. And with the hippos being moved so close to the house, he'd have plenty of chance to see them.

'Let's see what you managed to get, Jake,' said Brandon, as Sophie steered the jeep down the dirt track leading to the main gravel road that ran through Musabi. He rewound the tape and watched the reversed recording on the small LCD screen on the side of the camera. 'Right, here's where you took over,' he said after a minute and pressed the play button.

Jake leaned forward and looked over Brandon's shoulder at the segment he'd recorded. The screen was pretty small, but the colours were bright and the picture was quite clear.

'Hey! Not bad,' enthused Brandon as the camera lens seemed to swim through a gap between the bars on the truck then centred on the calf's face. The baby's pink cavernous mouth filled the screen, contrasting sharply with the next segment which showed the arid landscape. 'This is really neat,' said Brandon. 'You're going to love it, Sophie. It tells us the whole story and underlines the serious situation in the reserve without a word being said.' He switched off the camera and looked back over his shoulder. 'You're a natural, Jake.'

Coming from someone as famous and experienced as Brandon, the compliment gave Jake a rush of pleasure. But there was more to come.

'Say! How about you giving me a hand tomorrow when I go out on my bike to measure a cheetah's speed?' asked Brandon.

Jake was enormously flattered. 'Cool,' he responded. 'What do you want me to do?' He imagined it would be something like holding a stop watch while Brandon raced along on the bike. But he couldn't have been more wrong.

'After seeing your footage of the hippos, I think

I've just found my new cameraman,' declared Brandon. Jake waited, his heart pounding, to hear exactly what Brandon was planning.

'Which means that lets you off the hook, Sophie,' Brandon continued, smiling at his wife. He looked at Jake again. 'If it's OK with Rick and your mum, I'd like you to ride pillion and film the race,' were his next electrifying words.

TWO

Tambarare Duma – 5 kilometres read the carved wooden sign on the stone pillar at the side of the dirt road. It was early the next morning and the sun was rising in the east, painting Musabi with a golden-red light.

'Nearly there,' Jake said, barely able to hide his excitement at being so close to Tambarare Duma. The Swahili words meant Cheetah Plain and Jake could already see himself on the back of Brandon's bike racing across the open savannah with a cheetah sprinting parallel to them. He glanced over his shoulder at the trailer behind them. 'It's going to be awesome filming cheetahs racing against a bike,' he said quietly.

'*If* we see any,' came the sober remark of Jake's best friend, twelve-year-old Shani Rafiki. She had arrived just before dawn with her uncle, Rick's assistant Morgan, so that she could meet up with Brandon and Sophie again. Like Jake, she had helped out on the set of the lion movie and had become firm friends with the glamorous American couple. '*Dumas* aren't common like . . .' she pointed to a herd of warthogs scurrying away behind a bush, '. . . like *ngiris*.'

'I know. But we will find *dumas*.' Jake didn't even want to think they wouldn't. He'd lain awake half the night anticipating the day ahead – especially the bike ride. Even the short spin down a dirt road near the house yesterday afternoon had been thrilling enough. And that was without a cheetah running alongside! 'I've seen at least one cheetah at Tambarare Duma nearly every time I've been there,' he added confidently.

'I wish I could say the same thing,' said a tall young woman who was sitting in the back of the jeep between Jake and Shani. Her name was Frances Bury and she was a newly qualified game-ranger who had recently come from Zimbabwe to work at Musabi. With more and more tourists coming to the reserve, Rick and Morgan had their hands full so Frances had come to help out.

In the driver's seat, Brandon groaned. 'Don't say that. I've got my hopes pinned on things going well this morning.'

'You and Jake both,' chuckled Sophie. 'And mainly because you want to go chasing about on that bike, I'll bet.' She smiled at Shani and Frances. 'Boys and their toys!'

Frances tossed her long red-gold hair and laughed.

17

'I had a toy like that in Zim, so some of us girls wouldn't mind a ride on that bike.'

'You're welcome to it,' said Sophie. 'I'm just glad I don't have to cling onto the back while trying to film the race.'

'So who is?' asked Shani.

'Er . . .' Jake began but before he could continue, Sophie pointed into the distance and said breathlessly, 'Would you look at that!'

Expecting to see a cheetah, Jake stood up in the open-topped jeep and held onto the roll-over bar while scanning the horizon. But instead of a lithe feline shape, he saw a herd of ten elephants moving slowly across the plain in a single straight line about half a kilometre away. In front was an old female – the matriarch, the leader of the herd.

Jake recognised her immediately. After all, she was the one that had nearly flattened him on her way to rescue the baby elephant trapped in the mud. 'That's Rosa's herd,' he told the others. 'We brought them here from Lufubu Game Reserve in Zambia because they were breaking out through the fence and causing a lot of trouble.'

'What sort of trouble?' asked Brandon, slowing down for a better look at the elephants.

'Trampling fields and destroying crops,' said Shani.

Jake jumped to the elephants' defence. 'It wasn't their fault. Lufubu just couldn't support them any more. There were too many elephants and not enough water and vegetation for them all.'

'Sounds like a real mercy mission,' said Sophie.

'It was more than that,' said Shani. 'It was a family reunion.'

Sophie raised her eyebrows. 'In what way?'

Jake took up the story. 'There's an elephant here called Goliath. He came from Rungwa Wildlife Sanctuary two years before we brought Rosa here. He was always a loner and usually hung about near the house. We thought it was just because he'd been reared by humans and preferred them to elephants. But as soon as Rosa and the others were in the *boma*, he pitched up to check them out.'

'You should have seen it,' put in Shani. 'Goliath and Rosa were yelling and trumpeting the whole place down.'

'Yes, I heard about that,' said Frances, shifting the rifle that lay across her lap. 'It must have been an incredible sight.'

'It was,' said Jake. 'And it was even more incredible when it turned out that they were related. Mark, the vet from Lufubu, recognised Goliath from one of his tusks that sticks out to the side. He said that Rosa was Goliath's great-aunt and the last time they'd seen each other was about twelve years ago when Goliath was just a few months old. Someone found him standing next to his mother's body and took him to Rungwa. Then eventually, he came to us.'

'And they recognized each other after all that time,' said Sophie, her voice filled with wonder.

'I wish we'd been here to film that reunion,' said Brandon, accelerating again. 'That sounds really special.'

Not for the first time since he'd come to live at Musabi, Jake felt a rush of pride. To think that this amazing game reserve – a place where awesome things like elephant reunions happened – was his home! Still standing up in the jeep, he looked ahead. They were approaching Tambarare Duma, and the wide open plain stretched ahead of them and on either side of the road as far as the eye could see. Even in the drought, it was an awesome place. Herds of antelope dotted the landscape, cropping the short dry grass. There was even a pair of white rhino shambling across the plain like silent tanks on a military exercise, while overhead an eagle circled, looking for prey.

Whenever he saw an eagle, Jake thought of Bina, his tiny orphaned dik-dik. He and Rick had rescued her after a martial eagle had swooped down and taken her mother right in front of them. With Shani's help, Jake had hand-reared Bina and the little antelope was now strong and healthy, and as tame as any pet dog.

A sign on a stone pillar just ahead read: PRIVATE ROAD. NO ENTRY.

'Is that the service road your dad said we could use?' Brandon asked Jake.

'I think so,' Jake said and Brandon turned off the main road onto the narrow track.

There were a number of service roads like this in Musabi. They enabled the rangers to reach parts of the reserve not normally open to visitors, but Rick had given Sophie and Brandon special permission to use this one. The last thing they needed was for a crowd of tourists to gather around them while they were trying to make their documentary.

They bumped along the road for a while until they spotted a big herd of gazelles about a kilometre away. Raising the binoculars that hung round his neck, Jake recognised the distinctive markings of the Thompson's Gazelle – the horizontal jet-black band on the body and the white belly. The herd was well spread out, searching for grazing on the parched plain. They cropped the stubby grass, stopping at times to snap at the flies that settled on them, or to look round for signs of danger.

'Let's stop here,' Frances suggested. 'Tommies are a cheetah's favourite prey. We've as much chance of seeing a cheetah here as we have anywhere in the park.'

'But there's no shade here,' Shani pointed out. 'If we have to sit here and wait for a cheetah to walk past, we'll probably die of heatstroke.'

Sophie smiled at her. 'Don't worry. We've thought of that. There's a big umbrella on the trailer with the bike. And gallons of ice-cold water.'

While Shani and Sophie set up the umbrella next to the jeep, Jake and Frances helped Brandon to offload the bike. Brandon had just pushed down the bike's stand and when Shani whispered urgently, 'Cheetah. Behind us, to the left.'

Jake spun round. At first he couldn't see anything. But then his eyes were drawn to a dead tree that stood alone on the plain several hundred metres from the road. And there, sitting bolt upright in the thin strip of shade cast by the blackened trunk, was a cheetah, its attention fixed on the gazelles in the distance.

Jake's heart leapt as it did every time he saw one of the graceful cats. Here was the fastest animal on earth! And any minute now, he could be racing against it. As Jake watched, the cat stood up and stretched, then paced slowly forward, its eyes still glued on its prey.

'It's stalking,' Frances whispered.

Suddenly, everything started to happen at once.

Brandon tossed a crash helmet to Jake, crammed one on his own head and leaped onto the bike. He pushed the key into the ignition while calling across to Sophie, 'Quick! The camera.'

Sophie grabbed the digital video camera from the jeep and thrust it at Jake who quickly did up the strap of his helmet then swung himself onto the seat behind Brandon. As he did, he caught Shani's eye. She looked stunned.

'Hey! You didn't tell me you were doing the filming,' she said.

'Well, I . . . there wasn't, er, time,' Jake stammered, gripping the camera tightly in his right hand and clinging to the back of his seat with his left, ready for when Brandon started up the engine.

Jake felt a pang of guilt. He'd never got round to asking Rick or his mum. He didn't think they'd have objected, but he didn't think he could bear it if they said no. He shrugged at Shani. The sudden harsh noise startled both the cheetah and the Thompson's Gazelles. The antelopes jerked up their heads and stared at the bike, while the cheetah froze and studied the noise-maker intently.

'Don't move,' whispered Frances from just behind the bike.

They all stood still until the gazelles grew used to the puttering engine and went back to their grazing. The cheetah also soon lost interest in the noise and started to stalk the Tommies once more.

Brandon kicked the stand off the ground and rolled the bike forward. 'Let's go,' he said.

'Good luck,' said Sophie. 'And be careful.'

'We will be,' Jake told her. He put his feet on the footrests on either side of the back wheel. 'When should I start filming?' he asked Brandon.

'Right now,' Brandon said, grinning over his shoulder at him. 'We want all the action we can get.'

The cheetah was still some way behind them so

Jake had to twist round to get it in the viewfinder. Keeping the camera as steady as he could, he zoomed in on the stalking cat then gradually panned across the open plain, twisting himself to face the front again until he had the Tommies in view.

Brandon steered the bike along the dirt track, glancing behind from time-to-time to check on the cheetah's progress. Before long, the cheetah drew parallel with them, about two hundred metres away but moving slowly and steadily in the same direction. Through the viewfinder, Jake could clearly see the side of the cat's face, especially the trademark 'tear stain' of a cheetah – the black line that ran from the inside corner of the eye down the side of the nose to the cheetah's mouth. The big cat's eyes and the relaxed set of its jaws looked deceptively gentle, and Jake had to remind himself that the cheetah was on a mission to kill its next meal.

Concentrating hard, Jake filmed the slow, steady build-up to the deadly chase. At the moment, the cheetah was ambling forward casually, rather like a pet cat walking lazily to its food dish.

But Jake soon realised there was nothing haphazard about the cheetah's tactics, for whenever a gazelle looked in its direction, the careful hunter would drop to the ground and freeze, its pale yellow coat and dark spots merging at once with the mottled colours of the plain. Perfectly camouflaged, the cheetah waited patiently until the Tommy returned to its grazing, then it cautiously rose to its feet and loped forward again.

Gradually the unlikely pair closed in on the gazelles, the dirt-bike keeping pace with the fastest cat on earth. Trying to keep steady on the back of the bike as it bumped along the road, Jake held the cat in the viewfinder, wondering all the time when the cheetah would make its move. And when at last it did, Jake was quite unprepared. About three hundred metres from the Tommies, and with no warning at all, the cheetah suddenly exploded.

Brandon's reaction was just as fast. He accelerated immediately so that Jake was jerked backwards, the camera almost flying out of his hand. Suddenly the cheetah dropped to the ground. Brandon braked sharply and Jake lurched forward, slamming into Brandon's back and nearly dropping the video camera again. Quickly, he righted himself and pressed the pause button. 'Phew!' he breathed out loudly.

'You OK, Jake?' asked Brandon, putting his feet on the ground to balance the bike.

'Uh-huh,' Jake replied. He tightened his grip on the camera to make sure he was prepared for any more sudden movements.

'I hope he hasn't given up,' said Brandon, nodding to the cheetah who was crouched motionless on the dusty ground.

Jake remembered something Rick had told him.

Because they were sprinters and not runners, cheetahs couldn't go flat out for more than about three or four hundred metres. Any further and they would overheat dangerously. 'He probably realised he didn't judge the distance properly,' Jake told Brandon. 'He might start again when he's cooled down.'

Meanwhile, the gazelles seemed unaware of the danger they were in and tugged at the dry grass, their tails spinning ceaselessly.

With the engine quietly ticking over, Jake and Brandon sat on the bike and waited. The sun was now well above the horizon, making Tambarare Duma feel like the inside of a giant oven. Jake felt the backs of his legs sticking to the seat. He shifted slightly to unstick himself, being careful not to touch the hot exhaust pipe with his bare legs, then slipped the camera into his left hand so that he could wipe his sweating right palm on his shorts. He had just swapped the camera back to his right hand when the cheetah stood up.

'Here we go again,' said Brandon, twisting the throttle and lifting his feet off the ground.

Jake gripped the camera as tightly as he could. He released the pause button and began to film the cheetah stealing across the plain once more.

After a while, the big cat's gaze fell on a lone Tommy that had strayed to the edge of the herd. The cheetah started to move in on it in a deadly straight line. When the hunter was about a football field's length away, the gazelle turned its back on the cheetah, its guard well and truly down.

The cheetah saw its chance. In the blink of an eye, the cat became a spotted blur streaking across the plain as it torpedoed towards its victim. This time Jake was ready for the thrust of power when Brandon accelerated. The bike surged forward, its front wheel momentarily leaving the ground before hitting the earth hard again. Jake clung on while managing somehow to keep the cheetah in the viewfinder.

Just seconds into the chase, Brandon yelled out to Jake, 'He's doing nearly a hundred kilometres an hour!'

Sprinting at full speed, the cheetah hardly seemed to touch the ground. It flew across the savannah, reaching so far forward with its hind legs that its back feet hit the ground in front of its head, bending its body almost into a circle. Jake almost forgot to breathe. He'd never experienced anything so exciting in his life!

But the bike couldn't match the cheetah's rate of acceleration and quickly fell back so that Jake had to film the rest of the chase from behind.

When the cheetah was only moments away from its victim, the Tommy caught wind of it. The unlucky gazelle jerked its head up and looked round. Seeing the killer closing in, it sprang high into the air, then zig-zagged away.

But the cheetah was already hard on the Tommy's

heels. Like a heat-seeking missile, it pursued its target relentlessly. Using its outstretched tail like a rudder, the cheetah swerved and turned at the same time as its victim, kicking up puffs of dust each time its paws hit the ground.

Watching the life-and-death chase through the camera, Jake was beginning to think that the cheetah might lose the race if it went on any longer. But luck was not on the gazelle's side. Anticipating its victim's next turn, the cheetah cut the corner, struck out with a front paw and brought the Tommy crashing to the ground. A cloud of dust concealed the closing moments of the drama and when it settled moments later, the cheetah was lying alongside its kill, panting hard to cool down.

Brandon pulled up and switched off the bike's engine. 'That was incredible!' he exclaimed. 'That animal covered two hundred metres in about seven seconds. And it reached full speed in only half that time.'

Jake switched off the video camera. 'Nought to a hundred in three and a half seconds,' he said breathlessly. 'That's faster than a Ferrari!'

THREE

'You should have seen it. It was just a blur,' Jake told his mum and Rick late that afternoon when they were at the swimming pool. 'That poor Tommy stood no chance at all.'

After watching the cheetah drag its kill across the plain then disappear behind some boulders, Jake and the others had spent the rest of the morning looking for more action to film. But nothing else nearly as interesting had happened and they'd returned to the house with just the footage of the cheetah chase.

Rick swam to the side of the pool and pulled himself out, then sat on the paving next to Jake with his legs dangling in the water. 'I know it looks like cheetahs can outrun anything, but if you look at the stats, the Tommy stood a good chance of getting away. A cheetah's success rate is only about two in seven attempts.'

'So that means what we've got on film is pretty special,' said Sophie, who was relaxing on the steps in the shallow end with Brandon.

Hannah was lying on a reclining chair. 'I can't wait to see the rushes,' she said, sitting up. 'Why don't we go in to look at them now before supper?'

'Rushes?' Shani frowned. She was floating on an air mattress in the middle of the pool, her hands trailing in the water. She lifted her head so that the mattress bobbed about, slopping water over the sides. 'What do you mean?'

'Rushes mean the first footage of a film before it gets edited,' Sophie smiled.

Shani shook her head. 'English!' she said. 'It's a very weird language. One word can mean so many different things.'

'I know what you mean,' Brandon agreed. 'In America lots of words have very different meanings to what they have in England. Ask for jelly and custard and you'll end up with jam and custard!'

Shani pulled a face. 'Yuck!'

'It's not that bad,' said Frances who was swimming steadily back and forth, her lion's mane of hair caught up in a band on top of her head. 'Just add cake and cream and you've got trifle.'

'Trifle?' repeated Shani, looking more puzzled than ever as she slipped into the water to swim to the side.

Hannah laughed. 'We could go on like this for hours. Trifle is a pudding, Shani. I'll make you one at Christmas. But for now, let's stop dissecting the English language and have a look at the . . .' she paused and smiled at Shani again, '. . . the rushes.'

They went inside to change then gathered round the computer in Hannah's office to watch the video. Jake felt his stomach churn with excitement. He was pretty sure he'd managed to capture the whole chase. But was it good enough for a documentary that would be shown all over the world? Perhaps even good enough to win a famous prize?

Hannah linked the camera to the computer and clicked on the mouse. A close-up of the cheetah's face appeared on the screen then slowly gave way to a wider view of Tambarare Duma with the gazelles on the far side, while over the speakers came the gravelly roar of the dirt-bike.

Standing behind his mum's chair and watching the video footage unfold in front of him, Jake found himself reliving the chase. It was all there; the cheetah drawing parallel with the bike and its steady loping approach towards the Tommies; the careful hunter dropping to the ground and freezing whenever a gazelle glanced in its direction; and then . . . abrupt footage of the red dusty ground and the empty blue sky!

'That must have been when the cheetah took off the first time,' Jake muttered, trying to hide his embarrassment.

'It looks like it,' said Sophie who was standing next to Jake. 'But it's no big deal. We can edit that out easily. Let's hope the second dash comes out better.'

Jake nodded, feeling sick with nerves. He knew

how much Brandon and Sophie were counting on the video turning out well. What if he'd blown it and the rest of the footage wasn't good enough?

The lone gazelle appeared on the screen. Seconds later, the cat that was stalking it became a blur. But this time, it was not because of any fault of the cameraman. It was the cheetah's second attack.

'This is excellent!' Sophie exclaimed as the cheetah hurtled past the bike.

Over the speakers came the roar of the bike's engine and Brandon calling out the cheetah's speed, his voice muffled by the helmet but still sounding tense with excitement.

'Perfect,' said Brandon, exchanging a quick glance with Jake.

The camera wobbled once or twice but Jake had managed to keep the two animals in the picture for the whole thrilling race.

'This is as good as any cheetah chase I've seen,' Rick said at one point and Jake silently relished his stepdad's approval.

Finally, a long shot of the plain showed a cloud of dust billowing up in the distance, covering the two animals as the hunt reached a successful climax. Brandon's voice confirmed how fast the cheetah had covered two hundred metres and the screen fizzed into blackness.

There were murmurs of appreciation from the small audience clustered round the computer.

Hannah turned in her chair and looked up at Sophie, her blue eyes shining. 'A great start to your documentary,' she declared.

Sophie nodded. 'It's really neat, isn't it?'

'I don't know how you managed to cling to the bike and still get such good shots,' Hannah went on.

Sophie laughed. 'Luckily I didn't have to. Cling to the bike, that is,' She beamed at Jake. 'Thanks to Jake.'

Rick had been leaning over the back of Hannah's chair. Hearing Sophie's remark, he straightened up and spun round. 'Thanks to Jake?' he echoed, and without waiting for Sophie to answer, he went on, 'Don't tell me it was you on the back of that bike, Jake?'

Jake took a deep breath. 'Yes, it was,' he admitted.

Rick looked completely taken aback. 'You went out on a bike in the bush without asking me?'

Jake stared down at the floor but not before catching Shani's eye. She was looking at him as if to say, *I told you so!*

Rick took a step closer to Jake. 'I can't believe you're telling me this now.'

Jake shrugged but didn't take his eyes off the floor. 'It was no big deal,' he muttered.

'What do you mean, it was no big deal?' Rick shot back crossly. 'Of course it was. It was downright dangerous!'

'No, it wasn't,' retorted Jake. He looked up and met his stepfather's angry gaze. 'And anyway, nothing happened.' He glanced at Brandon. 'Did it?'

Brandon ran a hand through his hair. 'Sure, nothing went wrong, Jake. But it could have. And that's not really the point.' He spoke slowly and quietly, as if he was disappointed in Jake. 'I thought we'd agreed you'd speak to Rick about going on the bike.'

Jake could feel everyone looking at him. His face burned with embarrassment and anger. How could Rick tell him off like this in front of their friends? 'You're making a fuss about nothing,' he insisted. 'I know about the bush. And we were quite safe.'

'You know squat about the bush, Jake Berman!' said Rick.

Rick's words made Jake feel even more embarrassed. He appealed to Frances, hoping she'd back him up. 'We were a hundred per cent OK, weren't we, Frances?'

Frances raised both hands and shook her head, signalling to Jake that she didn't want to get involved in a family row. 'Sorry, Jake,' she said. 'You're on your own in this.'

Jake scowled. 'Well, it's too late. What's done is done.'

'That's right,' said Rick, his voice cold and hard. 'And that's why you won't be going out on any more film shoots.'

The words hit Jake like a sharp slap. 'You can't stop me,' he retorted. The video had been so good, Brandon and Sophie were sure to ask for his help again.

But as Jake looked pleadingly at Brandon, hoping he'd come to his defence, the American shook his head and said gently, 'I reckon your dad's right, Jake. I trusted you to ask permission. I never thought I'd need to check for myself.'

Jake was furious. Everyone was on Rick's side! He stomped over to the window and slumped into a chair then stared out at the garden, his arms folded tightly across his chest. He watched a black bird mobbing a small grey raptor, a black-shouldered kite that was perched in a tree. The bird kept diving onto the little kite which had to duck each time to avoid its tormentor. *It's just like Rick going on and on at me*, Jake thought sulkily.

Fed up with the other bird's aggressive display, the small kite took off from its perch and flew away. *And that's what I feel like doing*, Jake fumed. It had been the most brilliant day up till now. Trust Rick to go and spoil it all.

He looked back into the room. Apart from his mum and Rick, everyone else had left. They were watching Jake closely, as if waiting for him to apologise. But as far as Jake was concerned, he'd done nothing wrong. Rick was fussing about nothing as usual. He always acted like he was the only person in the world who knew how to survive in the bush. 'I'm not a two-year-old, you know,' Jake told his parents.

'Then don't behave like one,' said Rick, turning and heading for the door.

Jake could hardly believe his ears. 'I'm not,' he shouted to his stepfather's back.

'That's enough, Jake,' Hannah told him sternly.

But Jake couldn't resist taking a jab at Rick. He stood up and yelled. 'You think you're so great just because you know about animals. But you can't tell me what to do all the time. You're not my real dad!'

Rick paused and Jake sucked in his breath, waiting for what would come next. His stepdad just shook his head, then left the room without another word.

'How dare you speak to Rick like that?' Hannah gasped.

'It's his fault,' Jake insisted. In frustration, he kicked out at a footstool which slid across the floor, bumping into a pot plant. The pot tipped over, spilling dirt onto the wooden floor.

'Stop it!' ordered Hannah. 'And pick that up. Then go and apologise to Rick.'

Not until he apologises to me! Jake retorted silently. He yanked the pot upright and scooped up the soil with his hands. Then he brushed past his mother and stormed down the passage to his room. 'Grown ups!' he muttered, slamming his door behind him. 'They just don't understand.' He flopped down on his bed and stared up at the ceiling, his stomach churning. As far as he was concerned, he'd rather be sent back to England than apologise to Rick.

FOUR

Jake was starving when he woke up in the morning. He'd ignored his mum when she'd called him for dinner last night, deciding it was better to go to sleep hungry than to have to sit at the table with his stepfather.

He pulled on some clothes then walked quietly down the passage to the dining-room. *I hope Rick's gone out already*, he thought.

A half-empty jug of juice and some dried-out toast in the rack told Jake that someone had already been in for breakfast. 'Probably Sophie and Brandon,' he guessed as he tipped cornflakes into a bowl and poured milk onto them. He imagined the couple already arriving at Tambarare Duma looking for more cheetahs to film. Maybe Shani was with them. 'I should be there too,' he said through gritted teeth. 'How could Rick be so mean?' The bitter memory of last night's row took away his appetite. Half-heartedly he pushed the cereal around the bowl. 'I should have told Rick about the bike ride,' he admitted out loud.

'Yes. You should.'

'Shani! You didn't go after all,' Jake exclaimed in relief as his friend pulled out a chair and sat down. He'd been so preoccupied with his thoughts, he hadn't even heard her coming into the room.

'Go where?'

'Oh, you know. Home,' Jake answered quickly, not wanting to let on how bad he felt about missing that day's filming.

'But I'm not going home. I'm staying for the whole holiday, remember and going back to school with you next week,' said Shani.

'Of course,' replied Jake.

Shani looked round the table then picked up the cornflakes box. 'Is this all there is?'

'Looks like it,' said Jake.

Shani wrinkled her nose then poured out some of the flakes and drenched them in sugar.

'Have some cornflakes with your sugar,' Jake teased Shani.

'Well, you've got to give this stuff a taste, you know,' responded Shani, pouring milk into her dish. 'Otherwise you might as well eat dried-up leaves.'

'Come on! It's not that bad,' Jake laughed. Shani certainly had her own way of looking at things. And with her around, it wasn't easy to stay gloomy for too long.

'So what's the programme for today?' Shani asked, digging into the dish with her spoon.

Jake hadn't really thought about that yet. He'd been too busy thinking about what *wasn't* on the programme any more. 'Well, we could swim, or watch videos, or play tennis,' he suggested. Listing the options, he thought how boring they sounded in comparison to yesterday's awesome adventure. He sighed and punched the table with frustration. 'We should be out there with Brandon and Sophie looking for footage.'

'Well, we can't be,' said Shani sensibly. 'So we'll just have to think of something else.' She took a mouthful of cornflakes then grimaced as she swallowed. 'Just like I'll have to choose something else to eat. That's too sweet,' she said, pushing the bowl away.

'I tried to tell you that,' grinned Jake, echoing Shani's words. He stood up and went over to the French door to look out across the plains of Musabi. The drought was biting harder every day, but as far as Jake was concerned, even the tense, heavy atmosphere couldn't rob the reserve of its excitement. Out there in the wilderness were creatures of all kinds, from the 'Big Five' that the tourists pursued relentlessly – lions, elephants, rhinos, buffalos and leopards – to the tiniest of antelopes, the dik-diks and sunis, as well as the thousands of other fascinating creatures like bushbabies, chameleons and weird-looking insects.

And cheetahs too. 'I know!' Jake exclaimed. He spun around. 'Let's go for a bush walk, to look for cheetahs. If we find any, Rick would have to let us take Brandon and Sophie to film them. That way, we get to help with the documentary again.'

'Are you mad?' Shani accused him. 'If Rick finds out, he'll send you back to England.'

'No, he wouldn't,' Jake responded, hoping he sounded more confident than he felt. Before coming out to join his mum and Rick in Tanzania, Jake had lived with his gran in Oxford so that he could finish the school year. It was OK while he lived there, but suddenly he realised he couldn't imagine living anywhere else but in Africa, especially Musabi. 'Rick didn't say we couldn't go out for a walk.'

Shani was smearing a thick layer of butter onto one of the pieces of dried-out toast. 'No. But you know we're not supposed to go walking in the bush on our own.'

'So? We'll ask someone to go with us,' said Jake.

'Who? Rick?' Shani licked some butter off her finger.

'Of course not. And anyway, he's not here. He and Morgan have gone down to Chozi today,' said Jake. Chozi was a forested area of the reserve which had to be regularly monitored for snares.

'So that leaves your mum, the cook and—'

'And Frances,' Jake interrupted Shani. 'She'll come with us.' Frances was perfect, he realised. 'Rick won't be able to say a thing because she's a proper game ranger,' he added with satisfaction.

'OK. I'll go and find her while you make us a picnic,' said Shani. She pointed to the cold toast and the bowl of soggy cornflakes. 'And see if you can do better than that,' she chuckled.

Half an hour later, the three set off from the house. Jake had told his mum they were going for a walk with Frances and Hannah had okayed it. 'But no tricks this time, Jake,' she had warned, clearly still angry.

Anticipating a hot and thirsty walk, they each carried water bottles slung over their shoulders, while Jake had the extra burden of the picnic in a backpack. Frances was carrying her rifle which she held lightly in one hand at her side.

At the bottom of the driveway, Frances stopped. 'Which way?' she asked Jake, looking up and down the dirt road. She'd only been in Musabi a few weeks so wasn't very familiar without the layout of the reserve yet.

'Let's cross the river and go up to the plain on the other side,' suggested Jake. He pointed across the road to a river valley. On the far side, the land rose up steeply then levelled out to become wide grassland. 'It's not exactly like Tambarare Duma,' said Jake. 'But it's still the kind of open country cheetahs are supposed to like.'

'You never know. We could be lucky,' said Frances, crossing the road.

'Or unlucky,' put in Shani. She took a slug from her water bottle. 'Are you sure you want to do this, Jake?' she asked. 'It's stinking hot already. Just think what it's going to be like in a few hours time when we're out there in the boiling sun and there's no shade anywhere.'

Frances paused to coil up her hair, tucking it under her wide-brimmed khaki hat. 'Well, you know what they say about the English, don't you?' she said, winking at Shani.

Shani frowned and Frances went on. 'Mad dogs and Englishmen go out in the midday sun,' she said in a sing-song voice.

'Oh, that's so true,' laughed Shani.

But Jake was not to be outdone. 'Seeing as I'm the Englishman around here, you two must be the mad dogs,' was his immediate retort.

'Touché, Jake,' chuckled Frances.

They started down the rough slope towards the valley, their sturdy hiking boots crunching over the hard, rocky ground.

'Keep an eye open for snakes,' Frances warned.

Jake gave her a surprised look. He wasn't the least bothered by snakes. There were probably millions in Musabi but he'd hardly ever seen one. 'Snakes are more scared of us than we are of them,' he told Frances, repeating something Morgan had once told him. 'Most of the time, they hear you coming and get out of your way.'

'Not all snakes,' said Frances. She stopped and pushed down her thick sock to uncover her right ankle. 'See that?'

Jake could see two thickened scars just above the ankle bone. 'Fang marks?' he asked hesitantly.

'Uh-huh,' said Frances. 'Puff adder.'

Shani gasped, both hands flying up to her mouth. 'You were bitten by a puff adder and you're still alive!'

Frances pulled up her sock and walked on. 'Yep. A big, fat, lazy puff adder that heard me coming and *didn't* get out of the way.'

'It must have hurt a lot,' said Shani sympathetically.

'It wasn't just a sting,' Frances agreed. 'Luckily I wasn't too far from civilisation and got to hospital before the venom could do much harm. Still, I went through sheer hell for a while. So, to repeat what I said earlier,' she gave Jake a serious look, 'keep an eye open for snakes.'

'OK,' Jake promised fervently.

When they came to the river, they found that it was little more than a series of stagnant pools surrounded by smooth boulders. Jake noticed spoor marks on the stretch of sand next to the river bed. These showed that animals were still coming to drink. But how long would these few shallow pools last? And if they dried up altogether, what would happen then? Could the man-made water holes support all the game in the reserve? Jake wasn't sure.

Jumping across the boulders, they crossed to the other side of the river bed and scrambled up the steep bank. At the top, they surprised a herd of zebra that galloped off in a tight bunch. When they were at a safe distance, the zebras stopped and turned their inquisitive gaze on the intruders.

'I've never seen them looking so thin,' Shani observed quietly.

Jake noticed that the hipbones and ribs of some of the animals were sticking out sharply. The last time he had seen any zebras, they'd been plump and sleek like well-groomed ponies.

'You know things are bad when the zebras lose condition,' Frances remarked. 'They can normally cope with the tiniest amounts of food and water. But it's part of the natural rhythm. The rains will come back one day.'

'Doesn't feel like it,' said Shani grumpily, taking off her baseball cap and fanning herself with it. Jake nodded in agreement. This was his first experience of an African drought and he found it hard to share Frances's faith in the weather.

They set off across the empty brown plain. Everything was dead still and, unlike Tambarare Duma yesterday, there wasn't even a single antelope in sight. With his shirt drenched in sweat and the sun burning his legs and the back of his neck, Jake began to wonder if Shani hadn't been right. It was more than stinking hot out here on the open savannah. It was like being in a fire. Reluctantly, he admitted to himself that they'd be lucky to see anything other than the zebras today.

But just when he was about to suggest they turn back, Jake spotted a flock of vultures circling in the sky above them. 'I wonder what they're after?' he said as the huge birds began to glide to the ground not far away.

'A carcass, I expect,' said Frances. 'Let's find out for sure.'

Frances was right. Approaching the vultures, Jake peered at them through his binoculars and saw a dark heap on the ground. It was the remains of an animal; a drought victim, probably. 'I think it was a wildebeest,' he said, identifying the animal from its heavy blunt head. 'I guess it's only just died.' Apart from a missing foreleg, the carcass was still practically intact. That meant it hadn't been lying there long enough for four-legged scavengers like hyenas to find it.

'I'd say so too,' agreed Frances, lowering her binoculars. 'And it looks like it was pretty old. That's probably why it was still in Musabi and hadn't migrated north with the rest of the wildebeest.'

Jake hadn't seen the migration yet, but he'd heard all about it from Rick. At the end of the rainy season, as in some other parts of Africa, the wildebeest all travelled north to greener pastures, only returning to their southern ranges when the rains started again. Rick had described to Jake the incredible spectacle of thousands of wildebeest thundering across the plains, and Jake was longing to see it for himself. But with no sign of the rains, there seemed little likelihood of a return migration this year.

The vultures hissed and squawked excitedly as they tugged at the carcass. But when Jake and the others were just metres away, the ungainly long-necked birds flapped their massive wings and flew to the top of a dead fever tree.

'Sorry to disturb your meal,' Shani called to them. 'We won't be long.'

'Look, a jackal's pitched up for lunch too,' said Frances.

A golden jackal was lurking behind the trunk of the fever tree. With the vultures out of the way, the slim dog-like creature saw his chance and darted over to the carcass. He grabbed a chunk of meat, then, seeing the three humans coming closer, dashed back to the cover of the tree.

'There'll be no shortage of food for the carnivores if the drought doesn't break soon,' said Frances grimly as they passed the dead wildebeest and continued across the plain.

A heat haze blanketed the earth around them. The waves of radiation shimmered above the ground, like water glinting in the sun. *It's only a mirage*, Jake told himself, the watery vision suddenly making him feel very thirsty. He unscrewed the cap on his insulated water bottle and took a long drink of the ice-cold water. 'Mmm,' he said lowering the bottle from his mouth. 'Water never tasted so good.' He felt a jolt of sympathy for the unfortunate animals who had to rely on stagnant puddles in the river bed, or trek for miles to one of the artificial water holes.

The burning mirage grew more intense, layer upon layer of pure heat suffocating everything below it. And then came a new vision; a long, dark shape moving silently through the stifling haze as if it was floating just above the ground.

Just another mirage, Jake thought for a brief second. But he quickly realised that the mysterious rangy shape was not just an optical illusion. It was very real indeed.

'Cheetah!' he whispered, grabbing Frances's arm as the shape took form and he saw the long legs and deep chest of the phenomenal sprinter.

'Oh my,' breathed Frances. 'What incredible luck.'

The big cat was moving purposefully towards a busy area at the edge of the plain.

'It's carrying something,' Shani pointed out. Squinting against the harsh sun, she tried to make out what it was. 'Do you know what? I think it could be that wildebeest's leg.'

'It is too,' Jake said, looking through his binoculars.

'The cheetah must have brought the wildebeest down. And to get away from the scavengers, it grabbed the leg to eat it in peace somewhere else.'

Being careful to keep well back so that the chetah wouldn't pick up their scent, they hurried after the swiftly moving cat. Jake was elated. The scorching trek had been worth it, and with any luck, the cheetah would lead them right to its den. *I should have brought my camera*, Jake thought.

The cheetah ran up a short slope then paused and looked down to the other side. Moving as quietly as they could, Jake, Shani and Frances hurried over to a small hill opposite the slope. They hid behind a Mopane tree, peeping out at the side of the trunk to see what the cheetah was doing.

The cat looked around cautiously for a few moments before making a high-pitched chirping noise, rather like a bird calling.

'Now what?' whispered Jake.

The answer came just moments later – and it was more than Jake had hoped for in even his wildest dreams. As the cheetah continued to call out, three little spotted bundles emerged from a tall stand of grass at the bottom of the slope.

'Cubs!' exclaimed Jake. It was the first time he'd seen such young cheetahs. They already had the long legs and streamlined bodies of the world's fastest sprinter. But unlike their mother whose coat was flat and smooth, the cubs had pelts of long blue grey hair.

Jake guessed that this must be a way of camouflaging them while they were still so young.

The adult cheetah ran down the slope and dropped the wildebeest's leg onto the ground. Her hungry cubs pounced on it, bolting down mouthfuls of meat while their mother kept a lookout for danger.

Moving ultra-slowly, Jake, Shani and Frances edged closer. Some large boulders on the brow of the hill provided them with a perfect natural hide no more than twenty metres downwind from the cheetah family. Silently, they slipped among the sand-coloured rocks to watch the cats below them.

Crouching side-by-side, the cubs at in fits and starts, looking up nervously between mouthfuls. Jake noticed that the three ate in peace, never challenging one another for the best morsel. This surprised Jake. 'They've got good table manners,' he remarked, talking in a low voice. 'Not like lions.' He'd watched lions feeding on a number of occasions. Gathered around a carcass, a pride acted like a bunch of thugs, growling and snarling at each other, and engaging in what amounted to a feline version of fisticuffs.

'Compared to lions, these cubs are angels,' Shani agreed. She was sitting on her haunches behind a boulder and looking out from one side of it.

'Yes. For some reason, cheetahs are much more co-operative than lions when it comes to food,' said Frances. 'They're not even aggressive towards other big cats – which makes them prone to being chased out of their territory by bigger predators, unfortunately.'

Jake felt surprised. He had assumed that big cats shared their hunting grounds with each other, just like they let hyenas and jackals live in the same territory. After all, looking at the abundant herds of Tommies and zebras, you'd think there'd be enough prey to go around.

'Would lions and cheetahs get into a fight, then?' he asked.

Francs shook her head. 'No, I don't think a lion would take on a fully grown cheetah. And cheetahs tend to be good at avoiding confrontation. If this female felt threatened, she'd move her cubs to a different den. They move around so much, we'll be quite lucky to see them here again.'

'That seems a bit harsh,' Shani remarked, and Jake agreed. He looked back at the little family, and hoped they wouldn't be chased out of their cosy, sheltered den before they had a chance to grow stronger and develop their essential hunting skills – or at least before he had a chance to come back and see them again.

One of the cubs rose up on its hindquarters and tugged at the wildebeest's leg as if trying to tear off a big piece of meat. For a moment the young cat looked up the hill, and Jake found himself staring straight into the little animal's eyes. He froze, hoping the cub couldn't actually make out what he was. It would be a huge shame if the family got wind of the humans and ran off, thinking they posed the same threat as a jealous lion. And yet at the same time Jake felt enormously privileged to be making eye contact with a wild cheetah cub.

The little cat turned back again and tugged confidently at the leg, moving it just out of reach of the other cubs who instantly dived after it. The first cub dropped the leg and lay down to feed with its back towards its human audience for the first time.

And that's when Jake noticed that there was something very unusual about the cub. 'Hey!' he whispered, standing on his toes and peering over the top of his boulder for a better look. 'That one's got different markings.' He focussed his binoculars to make sure he had a sharp image.

Frances was kneeling behind a smaller rock to Jake's right. 'What do you mean, different markings?' she asked.

'Well, its spots aren't the same,' replied Jake. 'They're more like splotches, or ink-blots. And look at the stripes on its back.' Unlike its litter-mates, this cub had bold, unbroken stripes running the length of its spine.

'I see what you mean,' remarked Shani. 'Its coat is more like a leopard's.'

'Maybe it *is* a leopard cub,' suggested Jake. 'An orphaned one that the mother cheetah adopted.'

'Mmm. I don't know about that,' said Frances thoughtfully. 'Still, seeing as cheetahs aren't known to kill other cats' cubs, I guess it could happen that a female would adopt an orphan she came across.'

But when the cub looked round a moment later, Jake could see quite clearly the unique facial markings of a cheetah – the black tear stripes on either side of its broad nose.

Jake was completely mystified. Here was an animal that looked part cheetah and part leopard. 'That's it!' he declared in an excited whisper. 'It's a cross between a cheetah and a leopard! A *cheepard*!'

FIVE

'A cheepard,' repeated Frances. She shook her head. 'No, I don't think *that's* possible.'

'Well then, what?' asked Jake.

The cubs had finished eating and were trotting over to their mother, their little bellies stretched full. She sat up and began to groom each one in turn, licking their faces and necks clean.

When it was his turn, the cheepard had a go at preening his mother too while the other cubs tumbled playfully together.

'Maybe he's a sort of mutant?' Jake persisted. 'He's bigger than the others. And stronger too. Look, he's just knocked his mother over.'

Shani rejected the idea of a mutant straight away. 'Oh, come on, Jake. That sounds like something out of *Star Wars*! Your imagination's working overtime. It's just a plain ordinary cheetah with bigger spots.'

'Actually, I think Jake's on the right track,' put in Frances. 'But so are you, Shani.' She'd been kneeling on the ground but now she sat down and crossed her legs. Balancing her elbows on a rock in front of her, she studied the cheetahs through her binoculars. 'Sometimes a vary rare recessive gene crops up in cheetahs so that they end up with leopard-like spots and stripes down their spines.'

Shani made sure the cheetahs weren't looking in her direction then she quickly darted out from behind her rock and went to kneel down next to Frances. 'Are you saying we have found a mutant cheetah?'

'I wouldn't call it that,' said Frances. She looked across to Jake, her eyes filled with wonder. 'I think we've found a King Cheetah.'

'A King Cheetah!' Jake gasped. 'But they're incredibly rare, aren't they?' His mind flashed back to a website on cheetahs that he'd found on the internet while he was still in England. He'd almost forgotten about it, but now he recalled the few lines that described the King Cheetah, saying that it was the rarest of the big cats and was once thought to be nothing more than a myth. But research had shown that the animal did exist in parts of southern Africa.

Frances lifted her binoculars again. 'That's right. They're so rare that very few people have ever seen one.'

The mother cheetah had stretched out in a sliver of shade next to a thorn bush, her cubs resting at her side.

'Have you seen one before?' asked Shani.

Frances shook her head.

'Are you really sure it *is* one?' Shani continued.

'Well, I can't think what else it *could* be,' said Frances. She stood up slowly, being careful not to make any sudden movements. 'I think Rick should have a look at it. He'll know for sure. Let's go back and see if we can get a message through to him. I bet he'll be thrilled to have a King Cheetah at Musabi.'

Jake found himself wanting to protest. The King Cheetah was *his* find. It had nothing to do with Rick. And anyway, the whole point of looking for the cheetahs today was so that he could do something to help Brandon and Sophie. 'Rick probably won't be home until late,' he said quickly, crossing his fingers that this would be the case. 'I think we should tell Brandon and Sophie first. We can bring them back here to film the cheetahs. Rick can see them on the rushes later.'

'Mmm. I don't know about that.' Frances hesitated and Jake could tell that she was thinking about Rick banning him from going out on the film shoot. 'Let's see who we find when we get back to the house.'

'I wish they'd hurry up,' Jake said impatiently. 'It'll soon be too dark to go back to the cheetahs' den.'

He and Shani were waiting on the veranda for Sophie and Brandon to return. Frances had gone to her quarters to shower and change. Rick wasn't back yet either, and Hannah had left a note to say she'd gone to fetch some supplies from Sibiti. This was the nearest village to Musabi and it was also where Shani lived with her mum, the local midwife.

Jake looked at his watch. It was nearly four o'clock. There were probably *just* enough daylight hours left to find the den again – as long as they could get going very soon.

But there was no sign of Brandon and Sophie. Jake flopped down in a low wicker chair, his long legs stretched out in front of him. 'At this rate, we won't be able to go out again until tomorrow,' he complained.

'Well, they'll still look the same in the morning,' Shani pointed. 'Cheetahs never change their spots, you know. Not even King Cheetahs.' She was sitting on the floor, smoothing Bina's head. The little antelope stood very still with a blissful expression on her face.

'I think you're getting mixed up with leopards,' Jake replied.

Shani looked insulted. 'No I'm not,' she said indignantly. 'I wasn't the one who thought Cheepard was a leopard. I always knew he was a cheetah.'

'That's not what I'm talking about,' said Jake. 'It's what you said about cheetahs changing their spots. It should be, *leopards* never change their spots.'

'Why? What's the difference?' Shani frowned. 'They both have spots.'

'Never mind,' said Jake irritably. 'It's just a saying.'

He stood up, then paced back and forth, listening hard for a car engine.

Shani watched him for a while then said, 'Sheesh, Jake. You're so wound-up. Relax!'

'I *am* relaxed,' Jake shot back and sat down again.

'No, you're not,' argued Shani. 'Look at your leg. It's jigging.'

'That's just a reflex,' Jake defended himself. But Shani was right. Jake *was* feeling uptight. What if the mother cheetah moved her cubs to a new den before he had a chance to show them to Brandon and Sophie?'

'Let's have some ice cream,' suggested Shani, standing up.

'OK. I'll get it,' Jake offered, glad to have something to do.

'And while you're gone, I'll do a rain dance,' grinned Shani, stamping her feet on the ground and waving her arms above her head.

Jake shook his head. 'You look like a whirling dervish,' he joked. Leaving Shani to her comical dance, he went inside. A few minutes later he came back with two chocolate-coated ice creams, to find that Brandon and Sophie were coming up the driveway. Hannah was right behind them in her jeep.

'Rush hour,' Jake remarked, handing Shani her ice cream. 'I'd better help my mum bring in the shopping,' he said and headed out to the garage, gulping down his choc-ice so that he would have both hands free for carrying the parcels.

Shani followed him with Bina tripping along daintily at her heels, her head reaching no higher than Shani's calves.

'Had a good walk?' Hannah asked when she saw them coming over.

Jake opened the back of the jeep and took out a cardboard box filled with groceries. 'Yeah, great,' he answered, delaying the best news until Brandon and Sophie were close enough to hear it. They'd parked the jeep in the car port next to the garage and were busy unpacking their equipment. 'How was your day?' Jake called out to them. He tried to sound casual, but he was almost bursting with excitement.

'Oh, average,' replied Brandon. He picked up a cooler box in one hand and the digital video camera in the other. 'We only managed to get some background footage. No cheetahs today, so you didn't miss anything.'

Jake could tell that Brandon was trying to make him feel better about not being allowed out with them today. But after finding the King Cheetah cub, Jake had forgotten his disappointment, even though he still hadn't forgiven Rick for embarrassing him.

'Well, *you* missed something,' smiled Shani as the American couple came closer.

'What?' asked Sophie.

Jake couldn't hold the news in another second. 'A cheetah family,' he announced, the words tumbling out in a rush. 'A mother and her three cubs. And one of them was . . .' he paused and took a breath, '. . . a King Cheetah.'

The three adults stared at him in astonishment.

'Where?' asked Jake's mum, resting her box on the jeep's tailgate.

'On a plain on the other side of that river,' Jake said.

Hannah rested her eyebrows disbelievingly, which annoyed Jake intensely. Why couldn't his parents take him seriously for once?

'How do you know it was a King Cheetah?' she asked.

'By its markings, of course,' Jake told her.

'Yes, splotchy spots on its body and wide stripes running down its back,' Shani reported confidently.

'And also because Frances said it was a King Cheetah.' Jake gave his mum a meaningful look. 'She knows a lot about animals too, you know.'

Hannah returned Jake's look with one that warned him not to push his luck too far. 'I'm sure she does. But all the same, Rick will want to see the cub for himself.'

'Pardon my ignorance,' broke in Brandon. 'But what exactly *is* a King Cheetah?'

'It's a cheetah that's a leopard,' Shani answered promptly. Brandon and Sophie looked at her in complete confusion.

'I mean, its markings makes it look a bit like a leopard,' Shani explained.

'It's the rarest cat on the planet,' Jake added proudly. 'And to think it's right here in Musabi!' He shifted the heavy box in his arms then said to Sophie and Brandon, 'This could be exactly what you need to make your documentary really special.'

Sophie beamed at Jake, her eyes shining with excitement. 'The rarest cat on earth? You might have just struck gold for us, Jake! Do you think you'll be able to find the litter again?'

'I expect so,' Jake answered. 'As long as they don't move to another den in the meantime.'

'Why would they do that?' asked Brandon.

'Frances said there was a chance we wouldn't see the cheetahs again because they have to keep one step ahead of other predators, especially lions,' answered Shani.

'Sounds a bit stressful for a mother with three little cubs,' Sophie said sympathetically.

'Yeah. Nature can be very cruel,' Jake said. It wasn't until he had finished speaking that he realised he had just echoed a phrase that Rick used just about every day.

'The mother's probably still out hunting,' Jake whispered. It was early the next morning and they had returned to the spot where he, Shani and Frances had first seen the cheetahs. They'd positioned themselves behind the boulders while Brandon and Sophie set up a tripod in front of one of the rocks.

'I hope she doesn't take her time getting back,' said Shani. 'I've got to get a lift home with Uncle Morgan after lunch.' Shani's mum had phoned late yesterday afternoon to say that close friends from a village about fifty kilometres away had arrived unexpectedly to visit the Rafikis. The two families hadn't met up for years and were celebrating their reunion with a feast that night. Shani would come back to Musabi with Morgan the next morning.

Sophie fixed the digital camera onto the stand so that it pointed towards the area at the bottom of the slope. 'I hope she gets back real soon too,' she said. 'I can't wait to see the little ones.'

A light breeze rustled the grass where the three cubs had been hiding the day before, but apart from that, nothing moved. There was no sign of the baby cheetahs, not even a white-tipped tail sticking out from the clumps of grass.

'Are you absolutely sure this is where you saw them, Jake?' Rick asked after about ten minutes.

'Yes,' Jake replied irritably. He turned away from his stepdad and rolled his eyes at Shani. This was the second time Rick had asked him that. Why didn't he just believe Jake? 'I bet if you went down to the bottom of that slope, you'd find lots of cheetah spoor,' Jake added, beginning to wonder if the mother had moved the cubs after all. *If Rick hadn't come home so late yesterday afternoon*, he thought mutinously, *there'd have been enough time left to come back then.*

'You won't need to hunt for spoor,' Shani suddenly broke in. She was leaning over a rock, looking down the slope. 'The cubs are definitely there. I can see them in the grass.'

Jake peered through his binoculars. 'Where?' he asked, thinking Shani must be seeing things. But then he saw a small movement and concentrating on it, he quickly made out the round ears of one of the cubs. Thanks to its cape of long hair and its yellow-brown coat, it was almost completely invisible in the long grass. 'Yep. They're there all right,' Jake whispered triumphantly. Now it was just a matter of waiting patiently for the mother to return.

The minutes ticked by and the sun grew higher and hotter, but still the big cat didn't appear and her cubs stayed well hidden.

Hannah was leaning against one of the boulders, her camera at her side. Like Brandon and Sophie, she was keen to photograph the unique cub. She poured some water into the palm of one hand then splashed it onto her face. 'Will this ridiculous weather never change?' she sighed.

'It will one day,' Rick promised.

The air was hot and dry, and the ground burning to the touch, almost like melting tar or beach sand in the middle of a summer's day.

Rick sat down on his haunches. 'I hope you're right about the King Cheetah cub,' he said, glancing at Jake who was sitting cross-legged on the ground next to him. 'And that you haven't brought us all this way in this heat on a wild goose chase.'

Jake wanted to tell Rick that no one had forced him to come with them, but Frances spoke up first. 'I'm pretty certain it is a King Cheetah,' she said calmly.

Rick nodded then turned to Jake again and said softly so that the others couldn't hear him, 'By the way, there's something I've been meaning to ask you. What were you doing out here yesterday?'

'We were on a walk,' Jake replied. 'With Frances. And she had her rifle so we were quite safe,' he added quickly.

'That's not what I mean,' said Rick.

Jake frowned at him. 'What do you mean?'

'I mean, were you just out walking, or looking for ways of getting involved with the filming again?'

Jake felt like punching something. You'd think Rick would be *pleased* with him for finding something as rare as a King Cheetah. Instead, he was focussing on things that didn't matter at all. 'Can't I do *anything* in this place?' Jake said in an angry whisper.

Hannah glanced over to them. 'Anything wrong?' she asked innocently and Jake knew that she was trying to stop them from having another row.

'No. Just discussing the walk yesterday,' answered Rick.

Jake stood up. He wasn't going to discuss another thing with his grouchy stepdad. He slipped across to Frances who was sitting in the small circle of shade on one side of her boulder. 'Want a mint?' he offered, taking a roll of peppermints out of his pocket.

'Thanks, Jake,' she said, reaching for the mints. And in the same second she froze, her hand gripping Jake's. 'She's back,' she whispered, looking across the savannah.

Jake immediately crouched down and followed the ranger's gaze. His heart leapt when he spotted the cheetah running stealthily through the vibrating heat haze. As before, she was carrying something home to her cubs.

'What's she got this time?' Jake asked, freeing his hand from Frances's and lifting his binoculars.

'Keep still, Jake. She'll see you,' Rick hissed. Jake shot his stepdad a cold stare then focussed back on the mother cheetah.

'It looks like a Tommy,' whispered Shani.

Exactly as she'd done yesterday, the mother cheetah stopped when she was close to her den, then gave the bird-like call that would tell her cubs that she was home.

At once the three little cats burst out from their hiding-place and scrambled joyfully towards their mother.

Sophie quickly focussed the video camera. 'Aren't they the sweetest creatures?'

The mother cheetah dropped the carcass. Her babies pounced on it and, lying side-by-side, began to feed hungrily. It was easy now to see their markings – black tear stripes on their faces, the white tips of their tails, the spotted coats of two of them, and as clear as daylight, the blotches and broad stripes that set one cub apart from its siblings.

Jake stole a glance at his stepdad. Like everyone else, Rick was mesmerised. But then he looked over to Jake and, meeting his gaze, said, 'Well, Jake. You've found a King Cheetah for sure.'

Resisting the temptation to say, *I told you so*, and punch the air in triumph, Jake simply nodded at his stepdad then looked back at the cheetahs. The mother had joined her cubs now and was lying next to them tearing into the carcass.

'We should give them names,' suggested Shani who had slipped across to Jake and Frances. 'I guess we're going to be seeing a lot more of them.'

'OK,' Jake agreed. 'We'll stick with Cheepard for the King Cheetah. But do you have any ideas for the others?'

The cheetahs had eaten their full and Cheepard was stalking a lizard across a rock while the other two cubs started to play the cheetah version of tag – two spotted blurs racing after one another in a high-speed game that would help them to develop their hunting skills.

'Let's call the mother Kim,' suggested Shani. 'Short for *kimbio*, which is Swahili for *at full speed*.'

'Nice,' remarked Frances. 'And those two?' she asked, pointing at the tag-playing pair.

One of the cubs leapt onto the other, pushing it to the ground. The defeated animal, the smallest in the litter, lay in the grass on its back with the other standing proudly above it, its head held high. With its tear stripes looking like war paint, the young cheetah reminded Jake of a triumphant warrior. 'What's *tear* in Swahili?' Jake asked Shani.

'*Ufa*,' Shani told him.

'*Ufa* it is then,' said Jake, naming the second cub.

The smallest cub rolled over, kicking Ufa away. Ufa scampered over to Cheepard and joined in the lizard hunt. The lizard darted out of sight between two rocks and the cubs stared after it as if confused by its disappearance. Then Cheepard began to prod about with his front paws, trying to flush the lizard out from its hiding-place. His efforts paid off when the lizard suddenly reappeared and scurried across the rock towards the ground. In a flash Cheepard and Ufa were after it, their reflexes as keen as those of an adult cheetah.

For a while, the smallest cub watched them then yawned and stood up, stretching its long body to its full length.

'He looks like a piece of elastic being stretched out,' chuckled Shani.

'Stretch,' grinned Jake, watching the cub trotting across to join in the lizard chase. 'That's got to be his name!'

With the digital camera recording their every move, the cubs chased and sprang and boxed one another until at last they grew tired and lay down to rest next to their mother in the shade of a small shrub.

'They have no idea they've just become film stars,' Frances whispered to Jake.

Watching the tightly knit family, Jake wondered about the cubs' father. 'Does their dad have anything to do with them?' he asked Frances.

The game ranger shook her head. 'Very little. In fact, they've probably never even seen him.'

Jake felt a pang of sympathy. Like the cheetah cubs, he'd grown up without knowing his real father. He pictured the man named Greg who had died when Jake was only two, and whose photograph was in a frame next to his bed. *I wish he hadn't died*, Jake thought, fighting the lump that formed in his throat. He swallowed hard and in his mind's eye saw Greg standing exactly where Rick was, watching the cheetahs. That's what it would be like to have a real family. *It's just not fair*, Jake told himself.

SIX

Jake whizzed down the ramp on his skateboard and swooped up the other side. At the top, he leapt into the air and spun round in a half circle before zooming back down and up the far side again.

The ramp was at the bottom of the garden. Jake had made it himself, packing the ground down tightly with a heavy garden roller until it was hard enough to ride on. He'd worked on it every weekend when he was home from school and had only just finished building it, so that this morning was the first time he'd had a real go on it. *It's come out really well*, he congratulated himself. The ramp was smooth and fast, and at times it felt like he was flying.

Cresting the top of the ramp, Jake saw Shani and Morgan coming up the driveway in Morgan's truck. He sprang off the skateboard, flicking it up with a deft backward kick to catch it in one hand, then jumped down to the ground.

'How was the party?' he called out when Morgan had parked the truck and Shani climbed out.

'Boring,' said Shani, jogging across to Jake. 'Just a bunch of old fogies talking all night about relatives and the drought. They only listened to me once when—'

'Sounds really cool,' Jake teased, interrupting her. 'But here's something even more cool.' He offered Shani the skateboard. 'Want a ride?'

Shani stared at the steep ramp. 'Sheesh, Jake,' she said, appalled. 'Do you want to kill me or something?'

Jake laughed. 'It's really easy. Try it.'

'No way!' said Shani, taking a step back. 'I'd rather go into a lion's den than ride on that thing.'

'Yeah, I bet,' grinned Jake. Out of the corner of his eye, he saw Brandon and Sophie coming out of the house. They were carrying their camera equipment, ready for another day of filming. Jake would have liked nothing better than to go out cheetah hunting with them again, but he hadn't dared suggest it to Rick. He was sure the answer would still be no.

Brandon waved to Jake and Shani, then he stopped abruptly to put down the cooler box, said something to Sophie and hurried across the lawn. 'Is that a neat ramp or what?' he exclaimed, eyeing Jake's project with an envious look. 'Did you build it?'

'Uh-huh,' said Jake, trying to sound modest. 'Want to try it?'

'You bet!' said Brandon. He took the skateboard from Jake and climbed up to the top of the ramp.

'What on earth are you doing?' called Sophie, running over. 'Do you want to kill yourself?'

'That's just what I said!' chuckled Shani. Nudging Jake with her elbow, she grinned at Brandon and said to him, 'Now you're in trouble. You should have asked Sophie's permission to go on that thing. It's dangerous, you know!'

Jake and Brandon burst out laughing. 'Only you could get away with saying something like that, Shani,' Brandon told her. He stood on the skateboard, tested his balance, then pushed off and swooped down the steep incline. At the bottom of the dip, the nose of the skateboard suddenly dug into the ground and Brandon was thrown off. 'Ouch!' he exclaimed, landing hard on his side. He picked himself up and dusted the dirt off his legs. 'You were quite right, it is dangerous,' he said with a sheepish grin to Shani and Sophie. 'I should have listened to you.'

Shani's dark eyes twinkled with amusement. 'Yes, you should have,' she said playfully.

'Don't tell me you never get into trouble yourself,' continued Brandon, picking up his baseball cap.

'Oh, I do,' Shani answered. 'Last night, I was in big trouble for leaving the party and going to sit outside with Bweha.' Bweha, which meant jackal in Swahili, was Shani's mongrel dog. 'But it was so boring listening to everyone gossiping all night. The only interesting bit of the conversation was when I went inside again and told everyone about the King Cheetah cub. That's what I was going to tell you,

Jake, when you tried to make me have a ride on that thing.' She pointed to the skateboard ramp.

'Did they believe you?' Jake asked.

'Believe me?' repeated Shani. 'You bet they did. They almost fell off their chairs, they were so excited.'

Sophie had turned to go to the jeep but she stopped and said to Shani, 'Were they excited because King Cheetahs are so rare?'

'Yup,' said Shani. 'They were all just about passing out because no one from their tribe has seen a King Cheetah for years and years. They think that's why things have been so bad for them recently.'

'What do you mean?' Jake asked.

'I don't exactly know,' Shani confessed. 'Ordinary things going wrong, I guess. Like the drought, children getting sick, cattle being stolen . . . things like that.'

Brandon was listening carefully. 'So what you're saying,' he said, 'is that these people believe there's a link between King Cheetahs and the things that happen in everyday life.' He put on his baseball cap, then took off his sunglasses and cleaned them on the hem of his T-shirt while he listened to Shani's reply.

'Kind of,' said Shani. 'But not for everyone. Just their tribe, the Buhara people.'

'Go on,' said Sophie, sounding very interested.

Shani slapped a fly that had settled on her arm. 'Ugh!' She bent down and wiped her hand on the grass, then straightened up and continued with her

71

story. 'One of the grannies at my house last night told me that King Cheetahs are sacred in the Buhara tribal lands. They have lived there for thousands of years and have always protected the people. But there aren't any left there now.'

'So the King Cheetah's like some sort of lucky charm for them?' Jake suggested. He stood with one foot on his skateboard, pushing it back and forth across the baked earth.

Shani wrinkled her nose. 'I think it's more complicated than that.'

Sophie agreed with her. 'It sounds like they believe there's a mystical connection between their tribe and the King Cheetah. I've heard about that sort of thing before, like wolves or bears are totems for certain Native American tribes.'

'But Cheepard's at least fifty kilometres from their tribal area,' Jake argued. 'It's not like the people can see him regularly, and he can't be descended from their King Cheetah, can he? So why are they so excited about him?'

'I don't know,' answered Shani. 'But the granny said she was going straight back home to tell their witchdoctor, Mr Sangoma.'

'What can he do?' asked Jake.

Shani shrugged. 'I don't know. Maybe if he knows there's a King Cheetah around, he'll know what to say to the ancestors when he's praying, and what *dawa* to use.'

'*Dawa*?' echoed Sophie.

'Yes, you know, medicine,' Shani told her. 'Witchdoctors use traditional medicine – bark and plants and bones and things – for making things right.'

Brandon and Sophie looked more intrigued than ever. 'This is totally fascinating,' said Sophie. 'I mean, we just see a cute animal with an unusual coat. But for the Buhara, Cheepard has enormous significance.' Excitement made her voice higher-pitched. 'I think we've come across more than just a rare animal,' she said to Brandon. 'We've stumbled across a fascinating belief system. And in the centre of it, is an *incredible feline*.' She stressed the words that were the title of the documentary series she and Brandon were making.

'Yep. It sounds like the stuff of great documentaries,' said Brandon. 'We need to find out more. I think we should start by visiting the witchdoctor, this Mr, er . . .' He frowned, trying to recall the man's name.

'Sangoma,' Shani reminded him.

'Yeah, Mr Sangoma, that's it,' said Brandon. 'You coming with us, Jake and Shani?'

'You bet!' they said together, then Jake added, 'I'll just clear it with my mum, though.' He didn't feel like landing up in yet more trouble.

'And we'd better let Mr Sangoma know we're coming to see him,' said Brandon. He turned to Shani. 'How do we get hold of him?'

Shani looked surprised. 'By phone, of course.'

'Oh,' said Brandon, looking equally surprised. 'Somehow I didn't think he'd have one.'

'What do you think? That he'd use smoke signals?' grinned Shani. 'Or a runner?'

'They'd probably be a whole lot more reliable,' laughed Sophie. She took a small silver mobile phone out of her pocket. 'Look, no signal.'

'Not again,' laughed Jake, recalling the time he and Shani had first met Sophie. They were in the store in Sibiti to pick up some milk formula for Bina. Sophie had come in looking for a public telephone because her mobile couldn't pick up a signal.

'Modern technology's OK until it lets you down,' said Sophie, putting the mobile back in her pocket. 'Which often makes the old ways a lot better.'

Brandon winked at Shani. 'Perhaps we'd better use smoke signals after all!'

An hour and a half later, they arrived at the small village of Nareti at the edge of the Buhara tribal lands. Over the phone in Hannah's office, Mr Sangoma had explained where Jake and the others could find him. 'I have a small shop in Nareti,' he said. 'You can't miss it. It's the one without a sign outside.'

Jake didn't think to ask Mr Sangoma what kind of shop it was because he assumed it would be one selling traditional medicines. So when they drove into Nareti and Jake saw a low stucco building with heaps of herbs and bark displayed outside, he immediately assumed it was Mr Sangoma's store. 'There it is,' he pointed out to the others.

The shop was one of only three in the tiny village, a quiet dusty place that seemed almost deserted. The only people Jake could see were four men sitting on their haunches under a sick-looking tree playing some kind of game that involved bottle tops. 'Busy place,' Jake joked but he guessed that most people chose to stay at home, sheltering inside from the terrible heat.

The three shops were all on one side of the narrow dirt road – the only road in Nareti – while on the other side was the concrete block building that housed the local primary school.

'Looks like we've caused a bit of a disturbance,' said Sophie as Brandon pulled up opposite the school.

Dozens of curious young faces had suddenly appeared at the small square windows, while several children were standing in the doorway, some of them waving shyly to the newcomers.

Jake and Shani waved back until a cross-looking teacher came to the door, clapped his hands loudly and ushered his pupils back into the school room.

'I hope we didn't get them into trouble,' commented Shani.

With Jake leading the way, they went towards the

traditional medicine shop. Jake was about to go inside when Shani said, 'That's not it. It's got a sign.' She pointed to the home-painted board above the door. The large, uneven letters read, MR GANGA FUMBO – HERBALIST.

Jake was surprised. 'Does that mean there's a witchdoctor as well as a herbalist here?'

'What's wrong with that?' asked Shani.

Jake couldn't think of an answer, so he carried on to the next shop.

'This isn't it either,' said Sophie. A board advertising Coke and displaying the store's name, NARETI TRADING STORE was nailed to the wall. A speckled hen and her brood of tiny chicks were scratching about in the dirt outside the front door. Nearby, a big black he-goat was tethered to a bush. Having nibbled away most of the leaves, the goat was making short work of a brown paper bag that was caught up in the spiky branches of the bush. Like the children in the school, he stared inquisitively at Jake and the others as they walked past him.

The third shop was a narrow whitewashed building that, on the outside, gave no indication of what was sold there. 'This has got to be it,' said Jake, bracing himself for a store full of murky potions and strange powders. But when he ducked under the low doorway and saw what was inside, he found himself surprised yet again.

'Mobile phones!' he exclaimed. 'Mr Sangoma sells mobile phones.'

'And what's wrong with that?' Shani put her hands on her hips in mock indignation, though her brown eyes were sparkling with amusement.

'Nothing, I suppose,' Jake said. 'It's just that I thought Mr Sangoma . . .' He held up his hands. 'Never mind,' he muttered. It was too hot to get into a debate about a witchdoctor selling mobile phones in the middle of nowhere.

A deep, rich voice met them as they went inside. 'Good morning. You must be the people from Musabi.'

After all the surprises he'd had so far, Jake should have known better by now not to have any preconceived ideas about Mr Sangoma. But he did, and when he saw the person whose voice he'd just heard, he felt embarrassed by how wrong he'd been. Instead of a portly old man dressed in animal skins and surrounded by an air of mystery, Mr Sangoma turned out to be young, athletically built and wearing fashionable jeans and a T-shirt with a slogan on the front that said, *Sangoma for your Vodaphona*.

Brandon stepped forward to shake Mr Sangoma's hand. 'We're so glad to meet you,' he said warmly.

'And I you,' said the witchdoctor, his formal tone sounding almost old-fashioned, and a sharp contrast to his casual, modern clothes. 'I very much want you to tell me all about the King Cheetah cub.'

Jake grabbed the opportunity to describe Cheepard. 'He's really cool. Full of mischief and strong-looking already – a born hunter. And he's definitely a King Cheetah.' Jake stopped abruptly, suddenly feeling that he should introduce himself. 'I'm Jake Berman, by the way,' he said, extending his hand.

Mr Sangoma took Jake's hand and held it in a firm grip for a few seconds. 'I know,' he said. 'You look just as you sounded on the telephone.'

Jake exchanged a quick glance with Shani. What did the witchdoctor mean by that?

Mr Sangoma continued. 'I am glad you have come, Jake Berman. I have much to show you and your friends.'

'You have?' remarked Shani eagerly. 'What?'

The witchdoctor fixed his piercing dark eyes on her. 'Great things from our past,' he said, then lowering his voice he said with deep sadness, 'And terrible things too. Things of the present.' He picked up a bunch of keys from the counter. 'Come. I will take you to *Duma Mfalme*, our sacred site. The place where our ancestors walk with the spirit of the King Cheetah.'

SEVEN

Mr Sangoma led them out through the back of the shop to a small open-top red jeep that had seen better days. There was a dent in the front fender and Jake noticed that the front seats had sunk low as if they'd carried too much weight over a long period. The upholstery was cracked, reminding Jake of the cracks in the hippos' hides. This made him think of the suffering that the drought was causing, and he felt a sudden sympathy for the Buhara tribe's hopes that a King Cheetah could put an end to their problems.

'It will be best if we all go in my car,' said the witchdoctor, opening the driver's door. 'We do not like to trouble the ancestors with too much traffic.'

'Makes sense to me,' said Brandon. He opened the passenger door then pushed the front seat forward and squeezed himself behind it into the cramped space at the back. 'You sit up front with Mr Sangoma, Sophie,' he said, pulling the passenger seat back for her.

Jake and Shani climbed over the spare wheel on the tailboard and squashed up next to Brandon. 'Just as well we're all quite thin,' remarked Shani.

Mr Sangoma turned the key in the ignition. At first there was a feeble whining noise but Mr Sangoma persisted until a healthier roar came from under the bonnet.

This jeep needs a good service, Jake thought as Mr Sangoma reversed onto a narrow path that led round to the road in front.

'When I have time, I will take this jeep to Arusha for a good service,' said Mr Sangoma, looking in his rearview mirror and catching Jake's eye.

Jake felt startled – and rather uncomfortable. Was it just a coincidence, or had the witchdoctor read his mind? Whichever it was, he decided to think only good thoughts for the time they were with Mr Sangoma.

'Are you very busy in your shop at the moment?' Sophie asked Mr Sangoma.

'Not so much in the shop,' came the reply. 'But with my people. The times are bad and there is much hardship, especially for those who must live off the land. Once they grew all they needed, but we haven't had good rains for many years so there is nothing in the fields and the people must buy their food. With no money and no jobs, this is impossible of course. I am helping all I can.'

Does that mean he asks the ancestors for rain and things like that? Jake wondered to himself.

'The people come to me not just for spiritual guidance,' said Mr Sangoma so that Jake was now convinced the witchdoctor could see into his head, 'but also for financial help. And for lifts to the hospital in Arusha when someone is sick or injured. There is also the problem of cattle and goats being stolen by another tribe. I have to prepare special medicine then perform ceremonies at the *shambas* to keep the thieves away.'

'*Shamba*?' Brandon whispered to Shani. 'What's that?'

'A small farm,' she answered.

They joined the road and drove past the front of the witchdoctor's shop. Jake saw that the door was still as they'd left it – wide open. He was about to point this out when Mr Sangoma said, 'My shop is quite safe. No one will steal from me.'

Jake's jaw dropped open. This was getting creepy!

They left Nareti and were soon driving past fields of dried-out maize. Skinny cattle tugged hopefully at the withered stalks and black crows strutted about, cawing raucously and pecking at the ground. A group of women tilling the soil in a dry hot field looked up, then leaned on their hoes and waved as the red jeep went past.

'They live in hope,' commented Mr Sangoma. 'So they are preparing the land for planting.'

But to Jake, the situation looked utterly desperate. The fields were bare, the land baked hard, and every river they crossed was dry. And everywhere there were the skeletons – the remains of cattle that had succumbed to the drought and were not just heaps of bleached bones disintegrating under the burning sun. Buhara was practically a wasteland.

'It looks even worse here than in Musabi,' Jake remarked quietly.

Mr Sangoma looked at him again in the mirror. 'Indeed, those of us living today have never known a drought like this,' he said. 'Nor such hunger and poverty. And the Mgeni tribe that lives across the dry Katengeti river, who have left us in peace for many decades, are now the ones rustling our cattle. Evil has come upon us for the first time in many years.' His dark eyes glinted like coals glowing in a fire. 'But it will change very soon. This I have promised my people.'

Jake frowned at Shani. How could Mr Sangoma be so confident that things would soon get better? Just one look at this place was enough to make you think the exact opposite. He glanced at the rearview mirror, half-expecting the witchdoctor to have read his mind again and to make some comment. But this time, Mr Sangoma was silent.

They left the miserable farm lands and entered a rocky area. The road became narrower until it was no more than a track winding its way among huge boulders.

'Nearly there,' announced Mr Sangoma. He

changed to a lower gear as they started up a steep hill.

Jake wanted to stand up to see what was ahead. But wedged between Shani and the side of the jeep, and with his knees almost as high as his head, he could hardly move.

'Be patient a few more moments,' said Mr Sangoma.

This time, Jake simply stared in amazement at the witchdoctor.

At the top of the hill, Mr Sangoma stopped the jeep and they all climbed out. A wide plain stretched out below them, while behind was a rocky cliff.

'This is *Duma Mfalme*,' announced the witchdoctor with a broad sweep of his hand. 'It is the sacred place of the King Cheetah.'

They looked at the drought-ravaged savannah in front of them. Jake thought he could make out some antelope in the distance, but in the heat haze that warped the land, the shapes could have been bushes or rocks, or cattle.

'It's certainly ideal cheetah country,' said Sophie. She slipped the digital video camera off her shoulder. 'Do you mind if I get some footage of the area, Mr Sangoma?'

'Not at all,' replied the witchdoctor, much to Jake's surprise for he'd imagined the site was far too sacred to be filmed.

Sophie spent a few minutes filming the stark,

barren landscape. Mr Sangoma waited for her to finish, then he turned and walked towards the cliff behind them. 'Come with me now, please,' he said, glancing back over his shoulder. 'I want to show you the story of the Buhara people.'

Shani grabbed Jake's arm. 'Isn't this brilliant?' she whispered, her eyes shining with excitement.

Jake nodded. 'Kind of creepy too,' he said, then in the lowest whisper added, 'This guy can read minds.'

Shani gave him a withering look. 'Rubbish.'

'He can,' Jake insisted but there was no time to tell Shani about all the weird coincidences because the witchdoctor looked over his shoulder and beckoned to them before disappearing between two big boulders at the foot of the cliff.

They followed Mr Sangoma through the gap and found themselves inside a small dark cave. It was cool and dark in there – a welcome change from the violent heat and dazzling white light outside. But a heap of glowing coals in the middle of the floor provided some light and Jake soon made out two figures dressed in long black and yellow robes sitting on the ground next to the burning embers.

'I wonder who they are?' Jake whispered to Shani.

'And what this place is?' she whispered back.

'This is the cave of the ancestors,' announced Mr Sangoma. 'And these are the keepers of the cave.' He went over to the two people who nodded as he approached. Mr Sangoma knelt down next to them and spoke quietly for a moment, then he looked across to Jake and the others and said, 'Come. They will give you each a torch.'

The torches were burning sticks which the keepers lit over the coals and handed out to everyone.

'*Asanteni*,' said Jake as he took his torch. The ancient woman looked at him and smiled.

The other keeper was an equally ancient man who peered at Jake with old, tired eyes and said in a quavering voice, 'No, it is we who must thank you.'

'Really?' Jake couldn't think why.

'For finding the King Cheetah,' added the old man.

'Oh, right,' Jake said. He suddenly felt uneasy about how much the Buhara people seemed to value the little cub miles away in Musabi.

The witchdoctor held up his torch so that it shed a soft light in front of him. 'This way, please,' he said, walking through a small opening in the back wall of the cave.

Carrying their torches they followed him into a narrow passage.

'I can't imagine where this leads,' whispered Sophie behind Jake. 'Or what we're going to find in here. But whatever it is, this is just so exciting. I never thought for a minute we'd do more than look for animals on the savannah during this trip.'

'It's certainly more than we could have hoped for,'

agreed Brandon. 'Just make sure you get every bit of this on video, honey,' he said to Sophie.

'Oh, I am,' she reassured him.

'Can you film in the dark like this?' Jake asked her over his shoulder.

'Sure,' replied Sophie. 'The camera has a low-light function, so the torches will provide more than enough light.'

The passage was straight and level for a while, and its ceiling high, but after a sharp right turn it started to run steeply downhill.

Cautiously picking his way along behind the witchdoctor, Jake shone his torch down at the floor and saw that it was worn smooth as if trampled by thousands of feet over many years. He looked up at the rock ceiling and realised that it had got a lot lower, while the passage was also becoming narrower. He was on the point of feeling rather claustrophobic when the passage suddenly petered out and they were confronted by a wall of rock.

Now what? Jake thought, but the witchdoctor ducked through a tiny cleft in the rocks and when Jake went through after him, he gasped in amazement. 'Wow! It's another cave!' he exclaimed, his voice echoing around the empty chamber.

Jake felt as if he'd shrunk to the size of a midget. The cave was like being inside a huge cathedral. It was long and wide with a ceiling that towered high above the ground. A slender shaft of light shone through a hole in the roof to strike the wall on the far side of the cave, like a laser beam finding its mark.

'This is so cool!' Shani whispered, and her voice shushed and hissed as it bounced against the walls and travelled back to her. 'I've never been in such a big cave before.'

'Nor me,' said Jake, remembering the time he'd gone on a school trip in England to a system of caves in the Mendip Hills. That had been awesome, but this was something else altogether.

'This is the hall of the ancestors,' the witchdoctor told them, his deep voice resonating like a bass drum. He beckoned once more and led them over to the wall that was lit by the beam of light. And as they approached it, Jake realised why they were there. The wall was covered in paintings.

'Rock art,' he whispered to Shani, instinctively keeping his voice down. He'd seen a few rock paintings before underneath a rocky overhang in Musabi, but a closer look at these made him stop dead in his tracks. The paintings depicted lots of different scenarios but in all of them, one recurring feature stood out above everything else.

'King Cheetahs!' Jake gasped, forgetting to speak quietly.

Repeated over and over again in the drawings was the rangy feline form of a cheetah, one that wore the same splotches and stripes as Cheepard.

Brandon and Sophie looked equally blown away

by the unique sight. 'I can't believe our luck,' said Brandon, while next to him, Sophie panned slowly across the wall with the camera, making sure she filmed every single painting.

Mr Sangoma stood in front of the wall with his torch held high. The flickering light danced across the rock face and made the paintings look as if they were moving. Jake realised that this was exactly what the witchdoctor intended, for he was passing the torch deliberately across the frieze so that a story began to unfold.

'It's like watching a film,' Shani whispered to Jake, echoing his own thoughts.

Like an old-fashioned silent movie, the paintings revealed a sequence of events. A tribe of people working the fertile land, their children strong and thriving; great herds of cattle; good rains; healthy crops, and overlooking all this abundance, the King Cheetah.

Then came paintings of another tribe crossing a river, war paint on their faces, and spears in their hands. They surged up the river bank towards the first tribe who stood unarmed and looked down on them. And behind the peaceful tribe, standing tall and proud like a sentry, and painted as if he was much bigger than the people, was the towering figure of the King Cheetah.

The next sequence showed the warring tribe running back across the river while the first tribe knelt gratefully in front of the King Cheetah. Several more paintings followed, showing the King Cheetah watching over flourishing cattle, plentiful crops and a thriving community.

Coming to the end of the paintings, the witchdoctor looked round at his awestruck audience. 'This, before you, is the history of our people,' he said quietly. 'The paintings are thousands of years old so you can see that for centuries the King Cheetah has protected the Buhara tribe. Now I want to show you something else.' He walked across to a mound of rocks in the centre of the cave. 'This is all we have left of our protector,' he said, opening a wooden box that lay on top of the rocks.

Jake felt a shiver run down his spine as the witchdoctor took out a pelt. It was the pelt of an adult King Cheetah. *Surely they didn't kill him?* was Jake's immediate thought.

'This is the skin of the last King Cheetah that reigned here,' said Mr Sangoma. He draped it over his shoulders like a ceremonial garment, then looked directly into Jake's eyes and said, 'No one ever harmed him.'

The witchdoctor continued, turning to look into the camera lens. 'But one day when he was very old, he came into this cave and lay down and went to sleep forever. There was great mourning when we found him. He had been not only our protector but our friend too. So we kept what we could of him.'

He ran his hand across the pelt as if it was the most precious cloth in the world. 'Since then no new King Cheetah has come to take his place. And you saw for yourselves what is happening in this land.'

'But you said the people had hope and that things are going to get better,' Shani reminded him.

Mr Sangoma took the pelt off his shoulders and carefully laid it back inside the box. 'Indeed, we have great hope,' he said. A smile of joy spread across his face. 'You see, the King Cheetah has not forgotten us. He has sent us the cub you have seen in Msuabi.'

'This is utterly fascinating,' said Sophie, switching off the camera.

Jake was delighted to think that Musabi's own King Cheetah could bring the Buhara so much hope. But one thing continued to puzzle him. 'Cheepard's so far away from here,' he said to Mr Sangoma. 'It's not like he can even see you from Musabi. How can he possibly be your new protector?'

'That is why I need to see him for myself,' came the reply. 'Would your father mind if I came to see him tomorrow?'

'I don't think so,' Jake replied, too excited about everything to correct Mr Sangoma's mistake about his relationship with Rick. 'Come to Musabi in the morning and we'll take you to the den.'

EIGHT

'He is as I imagined,' the witchdoctor said to Jake, Shani and Frances. 'Strong, and already showing signs of being independent. I can sense the spirit of his ancestors all around him.'

They were walking back through the bush the following morning after observing the cheetah cubs for nearly an hour. In all that time, Mr Sangoma hadn't said a word. He'd kept his eyes on Cheepard as if he was hypnotised, never once looking away. Jake even began to wonder if the witchdoctor had gone into some kind of a trance.

'Are you sure Cheepard's related to the last King Cheetah that lived in the Buhara area?' asked Shani, taking off her cap and fanning herself with it.

'In that their spirits are connected, yes,' the witchdoctor replied solemnly. 'He's the chosen one. The one who brings good fortune to the Buhara.'

Jake couldn't help thinking that Mr Sangoma was being a bit optimistic. Cheepard must be two or three months old and so far, things hadn't exactly started getting better in the Buhara region. In fact they seemed to be going from bad to worse, if yesterday's trip through the miserable *shambas* had been anything to go by. And anyway, despite his special genes, Cheepard was just a playful cub. There was nothing mystical in the least about him.

The witchdoctor put a hand on Jake's shoulder. His touch was light, but a strange warmth flowed from his palm. 'You must have faith,' he said.

Jake was getting so used to Mr Sangoma's uncanny ability to see into his head that he simply nodded and said, 'I guess so.'

With Frances walking in front, they crossed the dried-up river bed and climbed the steep slope to the road in front of the house.

'What time will your father be back?' Mr Sangoma asked Jake as they approached the house. Shani and Frances were already some way ahead, eager for an ice-cold drink. It was yet another stifling day, hotter than before so that even the insulated bottles hadn't kept their water cold for long.

'Er, I don't know when Rick will be back,' Jake admitted. 'I didn't get a chance to speak to him before he took Sophie and Brandon to Rungwa this morning.'

Rungwa was the wildlife sanctuary where the elephant, Goliath, had come from. The animals that went there were usually either injured or rescued from captivity, or, as in Goliath's case, orphaned.

Mostly, they had to live out their days at Rungwa because they wouldn't have been able to survive on their own in the bush. But this morning, a pair of rehabilitated cheetahs were being released back into the wild, and Brandon and Sophie wanted to film the dramatic moment of their release. They had left with Rick at dawn, before Mr Sangoma had arrived.

The witchdoctor fixed Jake with his penetrating gaze. 'You have a problem with your father?' he asked.

Jake stopped in his tracks. 'Sheesh!' he exclaimed, surprising himself with Shani's expression. 'Do you know *everything* about me?'

Mr Sangoma smiled. 'Not everything. But I can see a lot in people's faces. And your face has just told me that you are not happy with your father.'

'He's not my father,' Jake said quickly. 'He's my *stepfather*. And sometimes he can be a real pain, like he's the only one who's allowed to know anything in Musabi. But it's OK, because I showed him I'm not so dumb. If it hadn't been for me, we wouldn't have found the King Cheetah.'

'Perhaps,' was all the witchdoctor said.

On the veranda, Shani was already delving into the bar fridge. She took out four Cokes and handed them round. Jake was just opening his when Hannah came out. She'd already met the witchdoctor when he arrived at the house earlier that morning. 'Did you see the cubs?' she asked.

'Yes. They were magnificent,' Mr Sangoma told her. 'Especially the King Cheetah cub.'

'Kim was there when we arrived,' put in Frances. 'Playing rough house with her cubs. As usual it was a real treat to watch them.'

'We've just been watching cheetahs too,' said Hannah.

'Really?' Jake said. 'Where?'

'In my study,' smiled his mum. 'We've been looking at the rushes of the cheetah release.'

'So Mr Berman is back,' remarked the witchdoctor.

'Yes. He came in about half an hour ago,' said Hannah. 'The release went really well, and Brandon and Sophie got some excellent footage for their documentary. It's gripping stuff. Come and have a look at it.'

'Sounds good,' said Frances, going inside.

But the witchdoctor had little interest in the video. He put his Coke can on the veranda wall and stood up straight, his expression serious. 'I would like to speak to Mr Berman, please,' he said to Hannah. 'I have something very important to discuss with him.'

'Oh, right,' answered Hannah, sounding a little puzzled. 'I'll call him for you.' She went inside and returned a few moments later with Rick.

The witchdoctor approached the game warden with his right hand outstretched. '*Jambo*, Mr Berman? *U mzima*?' he said to Rick, going through the formal greeting ritual.

'*Ni mizima,*' answered Rick, shaking the witchdoctor's hand the African way – a complicated three movement gesture that Jake was only just beginning to get right. 'We are all well here, thank you. *Habari ya safari?*'

'The safari to see the cheetahs was very good,' said the witchdoctor. 'The King Cheetah cub is like a miracle. Thank you for allowing me to see him.'

Rick smiled. 'No problem. That's part of what Musabi's all about. Being able to see wild animals in their natural habitat. You should bring your family next time.'

'Thank you. But that won't be necessary,' said the witchdoctor politely.

'Well, it's up to you,' responded Rick. 'But if you change your mind, just bring them along any time – although I can't guarantee we'll always be able to find this particular family of cheetahs. The mother could move them to another den at any time.'

'It is all right,' said Mr Sangoma. 'My family will have many opportunities to see the King Cheetah. And so will the rest of the Buhara tribe.'

What's he going on about? Jake wondered. *How can the Buhara people see Cheepard so far away? Unless Mr Sangoma's talking about them seeing his spirit or something.*

But in the next moment, Jake learnt that the witchdoctor had something a lot more practical in mind.

With the formalities now complete, Mr Sangoma fixed his dark brown gaze on Rick and announced, 'The King Cheetah is a gift to us from his ancestors, and I have come to take him home.'

'To Buhara?' Jake blurted out in disbelief. 'You can't! He lives here.'

'The King Cheetah belongs to us,' persisted the witchdoctor, still looking at Rick. 'I must take him back with me so that he can bring peace and prosperity to the Buhara people. He will be quite safe with us. We will build him a special enclosure at Duma Mfalme.'

Jake was speechless. To take Cheepard away from his family was totally unthinkable. He looked at Shani, expecting her to be just as shocked. She believed as much as Jake did that people shouldn't interfere with nature. But then he remembered how she'd been on the side of the villagers in Zambia when the elephants were destroying their crops. Would her sympathies lie now with the Buhara people? Or with Cheepard? But Shani didn't return his look. She simply stared at the ground so that Jake had no idea what she was thinking. He looked up at Rick, hoping like mad that his stepdad wouldn't agree to the witchdoctor's demand.

Rick folded his arms. 'I understand how important the King Cheetah is to your people,' he began calmly.

Jake's heart sank. Rick was going to let the witchdoctor take Cheepard away! Trust him to be so heartless. He appealed silently to his mum to put in a word for the cub, but she stood next to Rick, listening to the conversation and not looking even slightly anxious.

Rick hadn't finished yet. 'I'm sorry, Mr Sangoma,' he went on and Jake's hopes soared. 'But the cub stays where he is.'

'Yes!' exclaimed Jake and he punched his fist into the palm of his other hand.

Mr Sangoma looked taken aback. 'You cannot be serious,' he said.

'I am.' Rick's voice was quiet but firm. 'Regardless of his significance as a King Cheetah, that cub is a wild animal. He cannot be taken from his mother and kept in an enclosure.'

The witchdoctor slowly shook his head. 'My people are depending on him.'

'And he still depends on his mother,' put in Shani. Jake could have hugged her!

Mr Sangoma was not to be put off. 'Without this cub, the Buhara have no hope. Things are very hard, and getting worse every day.'

Rick nodded sympathetically. 'I know. But it is the same for everyone.' He turned his head and looked out across the arid lands of Musabi. 'The drought is everywhere. Animals are dying here every day, and on the road to Rungwa this morning, we saw dozens of *shambas* where nothing is growing and the people and cattle are suffering deeply.'

Jake looked at the can of Coke in his hand and felt guilty. Not only did he have something cold to drink, but he even had a choice of what to drink. Others weren't so lucky at all. Suddenly an idea came to him. *We helped the hippos*, he thought, then continued out loud, 'Isn't there any other way of helping the Buhara people? Like collecting food for them?'

'Actually, that's happening already,' Hannah told him. 'Shani's mum told me the other day that the government is rolling out a food relief programme in all the rural areas.'

Shani's mum ran the medicine clinic in Sibiti so was kept informed of any government health and welfare programmes.

'I know about that,' said the witchdoctor. 'But it is like putting a teaspoon of water into an empty well. We need something bigger, a miracle. Something that will bring the rain so that we can prepare for the future, and something that will stop the Mgeni tribe from stealing our cattle.'

Rick put one foot on the low veranda wall and leaned forward, looking up at the sky. High above, thin white clouds stretched through the air like delicate pieces of lace, but, being cirrus clouds, they held no promise of rain.

'There's nothing any of us can do to bring the rain,' he said. 'That's up to nature. But there is a way of dealing with the cattle rustling.' He looked over his shoulder at the witchdoctor. 'Have you contacted the stock theft unit at the police station?'

'Not yet,' came the reply. Mr Sangoma sounded sad and resigned to his tribe's fate.

'I think you should give them a chance to deal with it,' said Rick, putting his foot back on the floor.

'Perhaps you are right,' said Mr Sangoma. 'We didn't want to make too much trouble in case the Mgeni turned against us even more. But we cannot afford to lose any more cattle. I will call in at the police station on my way home.' He bowed his head to Hannah to signal that he was leaving. 'If you change your mind about the cub, you will tell me, won't you, Mr Berman?' he said, walking across the veranda.

'I won't lie to you,' Rick said, going down the steps with the witchdoctor. 'My mind's made up. The cub will not be leaving Musabi.'

Later that day, while he and Shani were swimming, Jake suddenly felt that he had to see Cheepard and his family again. 'Let's go back to the den,' he said.

Shani frowned. 'Why? We saw them just a few hours ago.'

Jake got out of the water and, without drying himself, hastily pulled on his shorts over his trunks. 'I know. But what if the mother decides to move them? We'll never see them again.'

'I bet that's not what you're really worried about,'

guessed Shani. She pulled herself out the deep end. 'You think Mr Sangoma is going to come back and steal Cheepard.'

Jake put his hands on his hips. 'I do not,' he said.

'Well, just so that you know, witchdoctors don't steal, ever,' said Shani, drying herself with a giant beach towel. 'They've got different ways of getting what they want.'

Jake felt alarmed. 'Do you think Mr Sangoma will get Cheepard in spite of what Rick said? Sort of spirit him away?'

'Not *that* definitely sounds like something out of *Star Wars*,' said Shani, shaking her head. 'And anyway, Mr Sangoma won't go behind your dad's back.'

'That's a relief,' Jake said. But he still couldn't get the cheetahs out of his mind, especially Cheepard. Every time he closed his eyes, he saw the little cub stalking the lizard across the rocks, or practising his hunting moves with his litter-mates. It was brilliant to know that such a rare animal lived in Musabi, and so close to the house, too. 'Come on, Shani,' he said. 'Be a sport. Let's go and see them.'

Like Jake, Shani pulled her clothes on over her wet swimming costume. 'We can't. No one's here to go with us,' she reminded Jake. After the witchdoctor had left, everyone else had gone out, leaving Jake and Shani to hold the fort. Hannah and Morgan had gone to inspect a bush camp in another part of the reserve to make sure it was ready for a group of tourists arriving the next day, while Brandon and Sophie had joined Rick and Frances who were transporting bales of hay to the hippos in their temporary water hole.

'That's OK,' said Jake. 'We'll go alone.'

Shani was appalled. 'You're mad! What if something happens?'

'It won't,' Jake said confidently. 'Every time we've been there, nothing remotely dangerous has cropped up. We'll be fine.'

Shani shook her head and sat down on a sun lounger. 'I'm not going.'

Jake shrugged. 'OK. Stay here if you like. But I'm going.' He pushed his feet into his rubber flip-flips then strode across the lawn.

'Hey! Wait for me,' yelled Shani, running after him. She caught up to him and said breathlessly, 'I'm not doing this for you. And if we get into trouble, it's your fault.' She fidgeted with her bead bracelet, a sign that she was troubled.

'I promise we'll be fine,' Jake said. He picked up a stick. 'Just in case we come across a snake or a lion,' he grinned.

'Fat help that will be,' Shani grinned back. 'Especially if you happen to stand on a puff adder.' She pointed to his flimsy flip-flops. Her own feet were well protected in a pair of strong trainers.

'Oh, all right, mother hen,' grinned Jake and ran inside to change into his hiking boots.

Taking their water bottles with them, the two friends set off for the cheetahs' den. Having been there three times, they knew the way like the backs of their hands so it took them only about half their usual time to get there.

'Didn't I tell you?' said Jake when they arrived safely at the rocky area where they always hid to watch the cats. 'Nothing to worry about. Not even a scorpion.'

'So far,' was all Shani said in reply.

They crouched behind a boulder and looked down the slope. There as no sign of the mother, but the cubs were out in the open, playing energetically. 'That's unusual,' Jake remarked. 'They normally hide when their mother's away.'

Shani shrugged. 'I guess they're growing up.'

Despite the sultry afternoon heat, the three little cheetahs raced about at top speed. They lashed out at each other with their front paws, pulling one another down like adult cheetahs bringing down their pray. Once, Cheepard grabbed Ufa's tail in his mouth and pulled on it hard. Ufa spun round and whacked her brother with her paw, managing to free herself at the same time. She flicked her white-tipped tail in defiance, then went to rest in the shade of an abandoned ant heap.

At once Stretch leapt onto Cheepard's back and sent him tumbling into the dust. The two lay still for a moment, panting heavily.

'Aren't you glad we came?' Jake whispered to Shani.

'I guess,' said Shani, grinning.

Jake held his breath as Cheepard stood up and shook the sand from his blue grey coat. Then he scrambled onto a rock and looked up at Jake, as if he knew he were being watched. The cub stood proudly like the King of the Castle until he spied a beetle scurrying across the ground below. He stared at it for a brief second before jumping down and zig-zagging after it.

Stretch had gone over to join Ufa in the shade. He flopped down next to her and playfully nibbled her neck.

'They're so . . .' Shani began then she froze, listening. 'What's that?'

'What?'

'The noise,' said Shani.

'What noise?'

And then Jake heard it. A deep, rumbling, purring sort of noise. It was coming from somewhere close by, perhaps even from behind one of the boulders. Jake guessed it was the cubs' mother. 'She must have seen us,' he whispered to Shani. 'Maybe she's warning us off.' Unafraid because he knew that cheetahs weren't usually aggressive towards humans, he peeped out in the direction of the noise, expecting to see the mother staring back at him. If he and Shani didn't make any sudden movements, the cheetah would probably leave them alone.

But Jake couldn't have been more wrong. It was not the mother cheetah returning to her den. It was something a lot more dangerous – a tawny, muscular creature moving stealthily through the boulders, intent on bringing death to the sheltered clearing.

'*Lion!*' Jake gasped.

NINE

Jake couldn't move. His heart thumped wildly in his chest and he felt the blood drain from his face as the dangerous creature came closer. It was the biggest lion Jake had ever seen, a huge male with a full black mane and powerful muscles that rippled as he walked. And he was heading straight for Jake and Shani.

The lion's rich, earthy smell wafted over to Jake and he realised with a tinge of hope that they were downwind of him. Maybe, just maybe, the dangerous cat didn't know they were there. Not daring to duck out of sight behind the boulder in case the lion spotted him moving, Jake could only stay utterly still and hope the beast would veer from its path.

Turn back, Jake willed him, clenching his fists so tightly that his nails dug into his palms.

The lion paused in front of a big flat rock, then jumped onto it and surveyed the scene before him as if he was looking for something. He held his broad heavy head high and panted with his mouth open so that Jake could see the four huge canine teeth that spelt death to any creature unlucky enough to find itself in the lion's clutches.

Jake's hands flew to his mouth. *Oh no! The cubs. He must have scented them!* He remembered Frances telling them how cheetahs had to keep one step ahead of other predators who wanted to keep the territory for themselves. The lion wasn't prepared to take on the mother, but he was happy to attack her innocent, defenceless cubs.

Jake's terrifying guess seemed to be spot on. All at once, the lion leapt off the boulder and bounded down the slope, straight towards the sleeping cheetah cubs.

'No!' cried Jake, standing up and scrambling across the rocks in a desperate attempt to do something – anything – to save the cubs.

'Come back!' Shani yelled to him. 'There's nothing you can do.'

But Jake could not go back. Every fibre in his body was driving him forward. 'Stop!' he shouted at the top of his voice, hoping that he might distract the lion and give the cubs a chance to flee.

But his desperate command was lost in the scorching air as the lion grabbed first Ufa, then Stretch and, right before Jake's eyes, snapped the little cubs' necks with a single crunch of its massive jaws.

'Run, Cheepard!' Jake screamed as the lion whirled round and with a mean, blood-curdling growl, charged the tiny King Cheetah.

Cheepard's flight reflex had already kicked in and he was on his paws sprinting towards a rocky outcrop a few metres away.

'Run!' yelled Jake again, but the lion was closing on the helpless cub.

Jake could hardly bear to look. As the lion skidded to a halt in front of the rocks, its massive feet stirred up a huge cloud of dust so that Jake was spared the horror of seeing the little cheetah he'd come to regard almost as his own being savagely mauled.

Jake felt as if a part of him had died too. Standing on a high rock, he glared down at the savage killer. 'You beast!' he roared out, matching the lion for pure rage. His voice rang out across Musabi like a siren warning of some terrible doom.

Behind him, he heard Shani calling to him urgently. 'Come back, Jake! *Please.*'

Jake ignored her, just as he ignored the tiny voice inside him that kept telling him that this was nature's way. 'You vicious, cruel brute,' he yelled as burning hot tears coursed uncontrollably down his cheeks. But Jake was too furious to feel embarrassed about crying in front of Shani.

The lion had been pawing at the ground but now he stopped and listened, turning his huge head to look back up the slope.

'Jake! Get off there,' shouted Shani.

Jake came to his senses at last. He dropped to his hands and knees and slipped backwards off the rock and onto the ground. But not before the lion had seen him. With a bone-chilling roar, the cub-killer spun round and powered up the slope.

Jake sprinted back through the boulders to Shani. 'Stand still,' he ordered breathlessly when he reached her, remembering Rick's advice never to run away from a charging lion. But it was too late. The lion's blood lust was roused. He was unstoppable and he rushed at them with deadly intent.

'We've had it!' Jake gasped, pushing Shani behind him as if he might be able to protect her. He looked round desperately and saw the only thing that offered any hope: the single Mopane tree a few metres away.

There as no time to tell Shani of his plan. In a last ditch effort to escape the lion, Jake grabbed Shani's arm and, in a split second, pulled her to the tree then shoved her roughly up the trunk. 'Hurry!' he urged her, already feeling the lion's hot breath on him.

Without a moment to spare, Jake leapt for a low-hanging branch. Clenching his teeth, he clung to it, desperately hoping it wouldn't snap in two and send him crashing to the ground. With his legs kicking beneath him, he swung from the branch, trying to find the strength to heave himself up.

An angry loud growl came from below. Out of the corner of his eye, Jake saw the lion leap up and lunge at him with a huge front paw.

'Watch out!' shrieked Shani from higher in the tree.

Instinctively, Jake jerked his legs up and screwed his eyes shut, expecting to feel sharp strong claws hooking into his calves at any second.

'Get on the branch!' yelled Shani.

With his arm muscles straining almost to breaking point, Jake pulled himself up until his stomach was on the branch. He wrapped his arms tightly around it then brought up first one leg, then the other until he was half-lying, half-kneeling on the branch.

'Keep going,' Shani called to him and Jake carefully manoeuvred himself along the swaying branch to where it joined the tree trunk, then stood up and climbed higher, scraping his shins painfully against the bark when his feet slipped against the tree trunk. As he pulled himself up to the next branch, he knocked loose the water bottle that had been attached to his belt.

The bottle plummeted to the ground, striking the lion's back on the way down. But the enraged cat barely noticed it, so intent was he on trying to pursue Jake and Shani into the tree.

Wedged at last in a fork in the trunk, Jake looked down. The lion was standing against the tree trunk on his hind legs, reaching up to his full height.

Snarling angrily, he hooked his front claws into the bark as if he was about to start climbing.

Please let Rick be right about lions not climbing trees, Jake prayed, while just above him, he heard Shani utter a strangled cry of terror.

The lion raked the trunk with his claws and made several attempts to pull himself up into the tree, but failed each time.

He's too heavy, Jake realised in relief.

The lion made one last effort to reach him, then gave up. He circled the tree once and, almost as if he was insulting Jake and Shani, lifted his tail and scent-marked the trunk before loping away.

For a while, Jake and Shani were too shocked to move or speak. Jake could only stare after the lion until the tawny muscular figure had vanished in the distance. Eventually he found his voice. 'I think it's OK to get down now,' he said hoarsely to Shani and, plucking up his courage, he climbed down to the ground.

'I hope so,' said Shani, not sounding at all convinced as she carefully followed him.

When he was on the ground Jake saw just how narrow his escape had been. The branch he'd grabbed was no more than two metres from the ground – not that much higher than Jake. It was probably just luck that the lion hadn't grabbed him and pulled him down. The realisation turned his legs to jelly. But another realisation, almost as bad as the first, now hit home in a big way. He'd been lucky. The cubs hadn't.

Choking back another rush of tears, Jake scrambled across the rocks. He had to see the little cheetahs, even if it meant his heart would break.

'Don't, Jake. There's nothing we can do for them now,' Shani called after him, her choked-up voice betraying her own heartache.

'I know,' said Jake. 'But I just want to look at them one last time.'

Steeling himself, he ran down the slope to where Ufa and Stretch lay. From a distance they looked as if they were curled up together, sleeping peacefully. *If only*, Jake thought to himself, and into a picture came his mind of the pair playing under the watchful gaze of their mother. *As if they didn't have a care in the world*, he told himself bitterly.

He reached the little bodies and flung himself down next to them, the tears streaming down his cheeks to soak into the dusty ground. The lifeless cubs lay in a crumpled heap, their bodies almost unmarked except for two deep gashes in their necks. The mark of the lion's teeth.

Jake leaned forward and lightly touched Ufa and Stretch, running his hands across their silky coats. They felt warm to the touch and Jake dared to hope that maybe, just maybe, they were still alive. He rested his hands on their chests, desperately wanting to feel a faint heartbeat.

Another hand reached out and touched the cubs. Shani's hands. She'd silently come down the slope too and was kneeling next to Jake. 'There is no pulse and no breathing,' she said quietly. 'Ufa and Stretch have left us. I think it was very quick. They wouldn't have felt anything.'

Jake looked away. He squeezed his eyes shut and bit his lip, trying to stop himself from sobbing out loud. *And Cheepard? Had he also died swiftly?*

As if a magnet was pulling him, Jake went over to where he'd last seen the King Cheetah cub. He scanned the area in front of the rocky outcrop, looking for the pathetic little body he knew would be lying there. But there was no sign of the cub. Only the scuffle marks on the ground and a number of large paw prints showed that a struggle had taken place there. *And it wasn't even a struggle really*, Jake told himself. *Just a one-sided attack.* Cheepard hadn't stood a chance.

Shani came over to Jake and looked around. Puzzled, she frowned at him, saying nothing, although written on her face was an unasked question.

'I don't know what happened either,' said Jake, baffled by the disappearance of the cub's body.

A horrified look stole across Shani's face. 'You don't think,' she gulped, 'that the lion . . . *ate* him?'

This was more than Jake could bear. 'No!' he declared. 'He *couldn't* have. Otherwise he'd have eaten Ufa and Stretch too.' But despite Jake's confident words, a grisly picture of the lion ripping the cub's body apart filled his mind. He tried to blank it out, but the nightmare image wouldn't fade. He sat on the ground and buried his face in his hands, thinking of the three little lives all snuffed out at once. 'Nature is so cruel,' he said miserably, using the same words he'd uttered to Sophie just a few days ago when they were talking about cheetahs having to keep out of the way of predators. And now, all too soon, he'd seen for himself just why.

An empty silence hung over the plain. It was as if Musabi was in shock after the savage killing. Gradually, though, Jake became aware of a noise close by. He looked up, half-expecting to see a flock of vultures descending on Ufa and Stretch. *They'd better not*, he thought grimly, bracing himself to chase away any scavengers.

But there was nothing there and the savannah echoed once more with silence.

Jake sighed, feeling a deep weariness settle upon him. 'I guess we'd better go back and tell everyone,' he said to Shani.

She nodded and they stood up, both glancing over to the two dead cubs one last time. As they walked away, Jake heard the noise again. It seemed vaguely familiar and was coming from somewhere near the rocky outcrop.

Jake turned round. There it was again – a chirping

sound, like a bird call or a . . . 'A cheetah's call,' Jake whispered. 'Like the sound Kim makes,' he reminded Shani.

'I can hear it too,' Shani whispered. 'It must be Kim.'

Jake suddenly wanted to run away as fast as he could. He couldn't bear to see the mother cheetah's distress when she found her dead babies. 'Let's go,' he said urgently to Shani.

But Shani was standing riveted to the spot, staring back towards the rocky outcrop where the lion had pounced on Cheepard.

'Let's go,' Jake implored her again, tugging at her arm.

'Look,' whispered Shani. 'In that crack in the rocks.'

'What is it?' Jake asked, squinting towards the outcrop. And then his heart leapt. A tiny face was peering out at them from the narrowest of gaps.

'Cheepard!' he breathed, hardly able to believe his eyes. 'He's alive!'

TEN

Jake ran towards home with Shani hard on his heels. He hardly noticed the thorns that ripped into his legs, nor the rocks he stumbled over. He didn't even look at the small herd of zebras that galloped away when he and Shani raced down a slope and startled them at the bottom. All he could think of was Cheepard, alone and without protection. If his mother came back soon, he might stand a chance. But in case Kim didn't return in time, Jake had to get help before the lion came back to finish off what he'd started.

Breathing hard, the two friends sprinted down to the dry river bed and bounded across the rocks to the other side, disturbing a monitor lizard that dived into one of the stagnant pools.

Shani paused to get her breath back, bending over with her hands on her knees. 'Wait a second,' she puffed to Jake who was already clambering up the hill towards the road.

'There's no time,' Jake called back. He felt a sharp jab in his neck and paused for just long enough to pull out a long thorn from an overhanging acacia branch before he raced on again. Coming to the road, he glanced over his shoulder and saw Shani about twenty metres behind. 'See you at the house,' he shouted to her. She'd be OK on her own now that they were so close to home.

Jake sprinted up the driveway, praying that someone was home. *Even Rick*, he said to himself, knowing deep down that his stepdad was the best person to deal with the situation.

With a single big leap, Jake bounded up the stairs to the veranda and burst through the screen door, calling out at the top of his voice, 'Rick! Mum! Anyone! Come quickly.'

There was no answer. The house was empty. Jake charged outside again, nearly falling over Bina at the bottom of the stairs. 'Sorry, little B,' he said, stooping briefly to pat her before heading for Rick's office.

Shani had just appeared at the top of the driveway. 'Where are you going?' she called to Jake.

'Rick's office,' he shouted back.

The office was a thatched rondavel near the back fence, and to Jake's enormous relief, Rick's Land Rover was parked outside.

With sweat pouring down his face, Jake rushed through the door. 'Rick! You have to come to the cheetahs' den.'

'What?' Rick whirled round to face him, looking

startled. He was standing in front of the fax machine, watching a fax that was coming through.

'It's Cheepard,' Jake panted. 'He needs us. A lion's just killed Stretch and Ufa.'

Rick stared at Jake. 'How do you—?'

'I'll tell you later,' Jake said. 'Please just come with me. Now,' he pleaded. 'Cheepard's in terrible danger.' He grabbed Rick's rifle that was standing against the wall and shoved it into his stepdad's hands. 'Let's go,' he said and ran out of the door, nearly colliding with Shani. Behind her were Brandon and Sophie.

'We're coming too,' said Sophie, and Jake saw that she looked ashen-faced. Shani must have bumped into her and Brandon on the way across the garden and filled them in on what had happened.

Not wanting to waste another second, Jake raced over to the driveway. He looked over his shoulder just once to make sure the others were following him then ran on again, ignoring the thirst that was growing in him. There would be plenty of time to drink gallons of water later when Cheepard was safe.

Safe? But how? How could they make sure the King Cheetah cub didn't end up as the lion's third victim? *We'll do something*, Jake vowed. Right now, the most important thing was to get back to the den as fast as he could.

With Jake sprinting ahead, they reached the

viewpoint at the top of the slope in record time. The sun was already sinking in the west. Soon it would drop below the horizon and darkness would quickly follow. Jake shuddered, knowing that night was when the predators came out in force – lions, leopards and hyenas, the most dangerous of them all. Unless his mother returned soon, Cheepard might need to be rescued before the keen-scented carnivores sniffed him out.

Jake scrambled down the slope to look for the little King Cheetah. Was he still hiding in the crack between the rocks?

'Wait, Jake!'

Rick's command stopped Jake in his tracks. *Surely he's not going to tell me not to interfere with nature!* Jake thought with frustration. After all, even Rick had softened when Bina's mother had been taken by the eagle. He had to see that Cheepard was just as helpless as the baby dik-dik had been.

'Come back up here, Jake, quickly,' Rick ordered in a tone that didn't invite any argument so that Jake reluctantly went back up the slope. He stood in front of his stepfather and said miserably, 'Now what?'

'Ssh,' whispered Rick. 'Get down.'

With that, a feeling of dread gripped Jake. The urgency in his stepdad's voice could mean only one thing. Something was out there. Was the lion coming back?

Jake crouched next to Rick and looked hopefully

at the rifle at his stepdad's side. If it was the lion, at least this time they could scare it off. He expected Rick to raise the gun, ready to fire a warning shot into the air. But Rick didn't even have a hand on the rifle. With a sinking heart, Jake believed the worst. Rick was going to let things run their course.

'You can't,' Jake began, but before he could continue his protest, he saw he'd been wrong. An animal *was* approaching the den. But it wasn't the lion.

'Kim!' Jake breathed softly, relief flooding through him.

As silently as the night, the mother cheetah streaked across the savannah towards them. From her mouth dangled the meal she'd brought for her cubs. This time, it was smaller than before – a hare – and Jake thought with a pang of bitterness that it was just as well Kim hadn't caught anything bigger. A gazelle would have been too much for one little cub. If, indeed, that one little cub was still where Jake had last seen him.

As usual, the mother cheetah paused and called out to her cubs, then padded down the slope, completely unaware of what she was about to find.

Jake herd Shani draw in her breath. He caught her eye and saw a look of pain on her face. Next to her, Sophie watched, wide-eyed and with her hands across her mouth, clearly also dreading the moment when Kim found her dead cubs. Brandon was holding the video camera ready. He hesitated as if he didn't want to record the tragic scene, then with a sigh, squared his shoulders and switched on the camera.

Kim stopped at the bottom of the slope. The gentle expression on her face gave way to a look of bewilderment, as if she was wondering why her cubs hadn't rushed out to meet her like they always did. She dropped the hare and sniffed the ground, then jerked up her head, her body suddenly tense.

Powerless to stop her, Jake wished Cheepard would come out from his hiding-place. Finding one cub alive might help to soften the blow for Kim.

But it was too late. In the dying light of the day, Kim had spotted her slain babies lying in the tall dry grass. She bounded over to them and sniffed their crumpled little bodies then licked them all over, nudging them gently with her nose as if urging them to get up.

Jake could hardly bear to watch. He wished he could tell Kim what had happened and that it had been very quick, and that he had tried to stop the lion. But maybe he hadn't done enough. Maybe he could have distracted the lion earlier and given the cubs a better chance to get away. And then a terrible thought seized him. What if he and Shani had somehow led the lion to the cheetahs' den? It had been so secret before the humans started visiting, laying trails of scent across the bush straight to the sheltered slope.

Filled with a mixture of guilt and confusion, Jake watched as Kim pawed at Ufa and Stretch. He heard Shani and Sophie crying very quietly, and out of the corner of his eye, he saw Brandon wipe away a tear that was rolling down his cheek.

At last Kim sat bolt upright, as slim as the shadow of the Mopane tree. And then came a sound like none other Jake had ever heard, a high-pitched keening that pierced the stillness of dusk and chilled Jake to the core as the distraught mother cheetah told Musabi of her loss.

The cat's heartbreaking wail echoed across the savannah before stopping abruptly. Kim bent down and gave her dead babies one last lick, then, without glancing back at them she moved away, a lonely figure heading into the silence.

Cheepard! Where are you? Jake wanted to run down to the rocky outcrop to look for the cub. The King Chetah cub *had* to be there. But why hadn't he come out when his mother had called?

Jake's mind fizzed with desperate questions. 'We must find Cheepard,' he whispered urgently to Rick.

Rick nodded. 'It's OK, son,' he began, and Jake stood up at once, ready to go and find the cub. But Rick grabbed his arm. 'No. It's OK, Jake. Look,' and when Jake peered into the fading light towards the place he'd last seen Cheepard, relief flooded through him. The last surviving cheetah cub was emerging from the cleft in the rocks to run after his mother.

'Thank heavens,' breathed Sophie.

Cheepard streaked after Kim who sensed her cub with the instinct of a heart-wrenched mother and whirled round to run back to him. Jake could almost feel Musabi letting out its breath when at last, mother and cub met and nuzzled and licked each other affectionately.

'She must be so relieved,' Jake whispered to Rick.

Jake's stepdad looked at him and said seriously, 'Yes. As much as any parent who'd found a lost child.'

Jake felt as if he'd been on a roller coaster of emotion that afternoon. Delight at seeing the three cubs playing, terror when the lion attacked, then sheer wretchedness, desperation and now, finally, despite the tragic deaths of Ufa and Stretch, relief that Cheepard was reunited with his mother.

Kim nudged Cheepard once more, then flicked her tail and, as if there was no time to waste, headed into the gathering darkness with her cub tumbling along at her heels.

'I guess she'll find a new den where Cheepard can be safe,' said Brandon, switching off the camera as the two cheetahs melted into the dusk.

'And we'd better get on home too,' said Rick, taking a torch out of his pocket. 'Lucky I grabbed this on my way out.'

But Jake insisted that they bury the dead cubs first. He couldn't bear to think of the hyenas or vultures finding them. Using the butt of his rifle, Rick scraped a hole in the ground, then he and Jake gently laid the limp bodies in it and covered them over.

'It's like when we buried the butchered chimps,' Jake whispered to Rick, remembering the other wretched burial he'd taken part in not so long ago. It was at a chimpanzee sanctuary in Uganda where an entire community of chimps had been massacred by bushmeat hunters.

With Ufa and Stretch laid to rest, Jake and the others stood silently at the side of the rough grave for a few moments before Rick said softly, 'Time to go.'

They started out for home, Jake trailing along at the back and glancing over his shoulder every few steps in case he caught a last fleeting glimpse of Kim and Cheepard.

When they came to the single Mopane tree that had been the saving of Jake and Shani just hours before, Rick bent down and picked something up. 'What's this?' He held up Jake's water bottle.

'Oh. That's mine,' Jake said, trying to sound casual while his mind raced to think of an excuse. He didn't want to let on to Rick about the narrow escape he and Shani had. If his stepdad knew, he'd probably drone on again about the dangers of the bush in an '*I told you so*' way. 'I, er . . .' Jake mumbled.

Rick narrowed his eyes at him. 'You lost it while you were up the tree? When the lion was here?'

'Yes,' said Jake, unable to say anything but the truth.

'Well, I'm relieved that's all that fell out of the tree,' Rick said meaningfully and tossed the water bottle to Jake before walking on again.

Jake felt a reluctant pang of gratitude to Rick for not asking any more questions. He slipped the strap of the water bottle over his shoulder then hurried on behind the others.

They'd gone only a short distance when the shrill unnerving laugh of a hyena came from somewhere behind them and, even more terrifying, the low, ominous rumbling of a lion.

There as no way of knowing exactly how close the big cat was, nor if it was the same one that had savaged Ufa and Stretch. But all the same, Jake began to feel a gnawing apprehension that made his stomach tighten. Just how safe was Cheepard in Musabi?

ELEVEN

Throughout the tough walk home in the dark, and then for much of the night, Jake couldn't get Cheepard out of his mind. No matter where Cheepard's mother took him, he would never be perfectly safe from lions and other predators. There were big cats all over Musabi.

In the morning, Jake was the first up. He went out onto the veranda and sat on the low wall. In the east, the red sky heralded yet another hot dry day. But Jake wasn't thinking of the drought any more. Cheepard was uppermost in his mind.

In the breaking day, Musabi looked completely peaceful. But Jake knew only too well that behind this veneer of peace lay a cruel, savage world, one in which tiny cheetah cubs were ruthlessly killed by bigger predators.

A flock of vultures was circling high above the plain across the river. By now, Jake's imagination was working over time. *What if something got Cheepard during the night and the vultures are about to . . .* He couldn't bear to finish the thought so he went inside to see if anyone else was up yet.

He found Rick and Hannah in the dining-room.

'You look as if you haven't slept a wink,' Jake's mum said when he walked in.

Jake shrugged and pulled out a chair. 'Yeah. I had a bit of a bad night.' He sat down and stared uninterested at the boxes of breakfast cereal on the table.

'Worrying about the cheetahs?' Rick asked.

Jake nodded. 'I wish we could do something to protect Cheepard.'

Rick took a sip from a mug of strong black coffee, then said quietly, 'We can't change things, Jake. Much as we'd like to.'

Jake lifted his head and glared at his stepdad. 'You always say that. But you *do* interfere. Often. Like when we saved Bina. And Rosa's herd. And the hippos the other day.'

'But those were all exceptional circumstances,' Rick said. 'And it's not as if we were playing Superman or anything. We were just helping to tide the animals over. Accommodating them for a short while.'

'Not Bina,' Jake argued. 'We took her out of the wild.'

'That's because she was a helpless orphan,' Hannah pointed out. 'And just sometimes, our sense of compassion tells us what to do.'

'Well, can't we be compassionate again?' Jake insisted. 'And rescue Cheepard?'

Rick leaned back in his chair. 'Rescue him? He's not an orphan, Jake.'

'No, but he's in danger,' Jake reminded his stepdad.

'No more and no less than usual,' responded Rick calmly. He stood up and stretched. 'See you both later. I'm taking the game guards to patrol the northern boundary today. We've heard that poachers have been spotted up there.' Unlike the other boundaries in Musabi, the one in the north was not fenced. This was to allow the wildebeest and other migrating animals to move freely between Musabi and the game reserves to the north. But it also meant that Rick and his staff had to keep a constant lookout for poachers crossing the border.

Rick kissed Hannah than put a hand on Jake's shoulder. 'Stay cool, Jake,' he said, before heading out of the room.

Stay cool! Jake echoed scornfully in his head. His stepfather was so cool he was practically an ice block. Jake never wanted to be as uncaring as him. He sighed with frustration and pushed back his chair.

'Not eating today, Jake?' Hannah asked.

Jake shook his head and was just getting up to leave when Sophie and Brandon came in. Shani was right behind them.

'Where are you going?' Shani asked Jake as he brushed past her.

'Dunno. Outside,' he said curtly.

Shani made a face. 'OK. OK. Sorry to upset you.'

'You didn't,' he said.

Brandon looked at Jake with understanding. 'It was a pretty rough day yesterday, wasn't it?'

Jake nodded and Brandon went on. 'Still, it ended well. Want to have a look at the rushes of Cheepard and his mom being reunited?'

'No thanks,' said Jake. 'I've seen it already. For real.' Ignoring the surprised looks from everyone, he went outside. The last thing he felt like was watching video footage of the cheetahs. Especially the part when Kim found the bodies of Ufa and Stretch. He never wanted to be reminded of that again.

He crossed the lawn and stood next to the fence that separated the garden from the wilderness on the other side. It was a world Rick insisted could not be changed, a world where animals killed each other for food, or even worse, to get rid of competition. A world where drought and poachers took the lives of hundreds of other creatures.

It's a hopeless place, Jake thought despondently. *And what's the point of making stupid documentaries? All the films in the world won't make things better.* He sat down and leaned against a tree, closing his eyes. He thought about the way his life had turned out and suddenly felt completely depressed. *I wish Mum had never met Rick, and that we'd never come to live in Africa.*

Oxford seemed a much kinder, safer place, a million miles away. Why couldn't he go back? He could always go to boarding school again. And in the holidays he could stay with his gran, just like before he came to Musabi. He could do normal things, like going to the movies, playing football and cricket, and going to burger bars with his friends. Who wanted to live in the bush anyway and see horrible massacres of helpless cubs, and animals dying from thirst and hunger?

A warm puff of air on his hand broke into Jake's thoughts. It was Bina, looking for a titbit. She must have followed Jake down from the house.

'Hello, little B,' he said, smoothing her head between the two tiny stumps that were her horns. 'I bet you're glad we interfered with nature and brought you here.'

He thought back to the days when he and Shani used to bottle feed Bina. Thinking about the tiny antelope also made him think about the baby chimpanzees he'd come to know in Uganda, who'd been orphans too.

'Just because you've been rescued doesn't mean things have gone out of balance in the wild,' Jake said, patting the baby dik-dik.

There was a rustling on the other side of the fence. Jake peered through the dense undergrowth and saw a big bulky grey shape coming towards him. 'Goliath?' he called. 'Is that you?' He hoped it was. Goliath was probably the only elephant in Musabi that Jake didn't mind getting too close to. This was because the young bull elephant had been raised by keepers at the Rungwa Sanctuary so he was relaxed around humans.

Moments later a familiar face emerged from the bushes. 'It is you, Goliath,' said Jake in relief, recognizing his old friend at once by his right-angled tusk. 'What's up?'

Goliath lifted his trunk high and tried to reach over the fence.

Despite his gloomy mood, Jake laughed. 'It's no use trying to cadge bananas off me any more, Gol. You're supposed to fend for yourself now.' He pushed himself to his feet and reached up to touch Goliath's trunk. 'I haven't seen you for ages. How are you?' It wasn't all that long ago that the elephant used to hang around the fence almost every day, looking for his favourite treat. But that was before he met up with his great-aunt, Rosa. Thanks to the old matriarch, Goliath's solitary days were now over and he had teamed up with some other young bachelor elephants that had come to Musabi with Rosa's herd.

And all because a bunch of humans went down to Zambia to rescue them, Jake thought. He pushed aside Goliath's searching trunk. 'It doesn't matter what Rick says. We've done a lot to make things better for the animals,' Jake muttered out loud as if he was discussing the issue with Bina and Goliath. 'And I bet we could make things safer for Cheepard too.'

'How?' said a voice behind Jake.

He turned round and saw Shani coming over. 'Well, by keeping him in a safe place for a start.'

'Like Mr Sangoma's enclosure up at Duma Mfalme?' said Shani quietly.

'Yeah, why not?' Just a few days ago, the idea of Cheepard behind bars had been unthinkable, but now it was beginning to look a pretty good option. 'At least that way he'd be safe from lions.'

'And everything else,' Shani butted in. 'He'd never had a normal life.'

'What's so great about a normal life?' Jake retorted, forgetting that only moments ago he'd wished he could have a normal life again. 'When it means you could get killed at any time?'

'But it's the way of the wild,' Shani insisted. 'And you know yourself that wild animals should be free. Just think about Marmaduke and Marigold, and what it would have been like for them if Mr Alderton had taken them to America.'

Hank Alderton was the producer of the lion movie that had been filmed in Musabi. At first, he'd planned to take the two cubs, Marigold and Marmaduke, back to America when filming was finished, but Brandon and Sophie, with the help of Jake and Shani, had changed his mind.

'Yeah, well, Cheepard would still be in Africa and he'd be safe as well,' Jake argued. 'I think Mr Sangoma *should* come and take him away after all.'

Shani's eyes grew wide. 'You're crazy, Jake.

Cheepard must be left alone. Like your dad said.'

'Stop calling him my dad,' Jake shot back, annoyed that Shani kept backing up Rick. Why couldn't she see the other side of things? Especially after she'd watched the lion brutally killing Ufa and Stretch – and nearly copped it herself when the lion charged her and Jake.

Thoroughly fed up with everyone, not least with Shani who was supposed to be his friend, Jake stomped back to the house in a huff. He went into his bedroom and lay on his bed, staring up at the ceiling. The only thing in his mind now was the safety that Mr Sangoma's enclosure offered Cheepard.

This gave him an idea. *I'll phone the witchdoctor and tell him what's happened. If he knows that Cheepard's in big danger, he'll definitely want to take him away, and he might end up persuading Rick*. Jake could see no flaws in the plan. After all, Mr Sangoma and the Buhara people were in the area long before Rick so they should have more say in things.

Jake got up and went into Hannah's office. Luckily, she wasn't there and he rifled through the telephone directory looking for Mr Sangoma's details. He found the number and quickly dialled it, keeping watch through the open door in case his mum came in.

The phone rang for ages and Jake was on the point of hanging up when Mr Sangoma answered.

'Sangoma for your vodaphona,' said the witchdoctor

in a sing-song voice. 'What can I do for you?'

Without even saying who he was, Jake blurted out urgently, 'You must come and take Cheepard away. It's very important.'

'Jake? Is that you?'

'Yes. Look, I can't explain now. But come to Musabi as soon as you can. I'll tell you everything then,' said Jake, hearing footsteps in the passage.

'But this is very sudden,' said Mr Sangoma. 'What has happened?'

'Can't talk now. Come tomorrow morning,' said Jake, hanging up.

'Elephants! At the pool.' Jake charged into Rick and Hannah's bedroom at dawn the next morning.

'What?' Rick sat up, forcing his eyes open. 'What are you on about, Jake?'

'Elephants at the swimming pool,' Jake said again. 'I think they've come to drink.'

Rick shot out of bed. 'How the hell did they get there?' he said, shoving on his boots.

'They must have pushed the fence down,' Jake guessed.

A loud trumpeting broke out. It was so close it sounded like it was just outside the window.

'You're not joking, are you!' exclaimed Rick, running out of the door after Jake.

They charged down the passage, meeting Brandon and Sophie, who were looking very surprised.

'It sounds like there's a herd of elephants in the garden,' said Sophie, just as Shani emerged from her bedroom, rubbing her eyes.

'I can hear elephants,' she said. 'I think they're outside.'

'They are,' Jake told her.

They rushed out, everyone still in their pyjamas – except for Jake who'd been up for nearly an hour already. When they were near the pool, they all skidded to a halt and stared in amazement.

Three elephants had come to the swimming pool. Two of them were standing next to the deep end, dipping their trunks below the surface. They sucked up gallons of water then, using their trunks like hose pipes, sprayed themselves all over. The third elephant was standing ankle-deep on the top step in the shallow end. He swung his trunk back and forth, splashing sheets of water onto the paving.

'Sheesh!' exclaimed Shani. 'There's going to be no water left in the pool soon.'

'And what would be worse is if that big fellow gets into it,' Rick said grimly. 'We'd have a hell of a job getting him out again.'

Brandon, never without the video camera, was already filming the extraordinary event. 'Aren't they having the best of times?' he chuckled. 'And it's a great piece of comedy. Perfect for the documentary. It'll help to lift the mood after all the tough drought-related footage we have.'

'It might *look* funny,' said Rick who was obviously not at all impressed by the elephants' antics. 'But it's not going to be funny when we try to chase them off.'

The elephant on the steps swung his huge head round to look at his audience. Facing them head on for the first time, he gave away his identity. His left tusk jutted out at a right angle.

'It's Goliath,' Jake said with some relief. 'So that's what he was doing here yesterday. Deciding on a way in.'

'Well, he can decide on a way out now,' said Hannah. 'There are plenty of boreholes in the reserve for him and his chums.'

'Stay back, everyone,' ordered Rick. He strode towards the elephants, waving his arms at them. 'Oy, you lot! Get out!'

Goliath and his fellows stared calmly at Rick.

'Go on!' said Rick, clapping his hands and going closer.

Jake and the others had retreated to the veranda.

'Is that safe, the way Rick's approaching them?' Sophie asked anxiously.

'Probably not for the average person,' answered Hannah. 'But I think Rick knows what he's doing.'

Rick continued to wave his arms while shouting, 'Scram, Goliath!' but the young bull wasn't in the least ruffled. He siphoned up some water then pointed his trunk towards Rick.

'Watch out!' Shani called just as Goliath squirted a jet of water at Rick.

Too late. Rick was drenched from head to foot. 'You devil!' he exclaimed but Jake could tell from his voice that his stepdad wasn't too annoyed. And to Goliath, the whole thing was probably just a big game. Jake was even sure he could see a mischievous twinkle in the elephant's eyes.

For fifteen minutes, Rick tried to persuade the elephants to leave the pool. But the three bulls made it quite plain that they weren't leaving. They stood their ground, refusing to budge an inch while splashing water everywhere. Already the water level in the pool had dropped considerably.

Rick eventually came back to the veranda. 'I might have to try a few gun shots,' he said, wiping his sweating forehead. 'Trouble with that, though, is it could make them stampede.'

'Oh, great,' remarked Hannah. 'Elephants stampeding through my garden and into the house. Just what I always wanted!'

Shani was sitting on the low wall with her legs dangling down. 'I've got an idea,' she said. 'Bananas.'

'Cool!' said Jake enthusiastically, guessing what Shani was thinking. 'That'll get Goliath moving.'

Sophie and Brandon looked perplexed. 'How will bananas help?' asked Brandon.

'We'll lure Goliath away with them,' said Jake.

'It's worth a try, I suppose,' said Rick.

While Rick went to find where the elephants had got in, Jake fetched some bananas from the kitchen. Then, armed with the fruit, he and Shani started to entice Goliath and his friends away from the pool.

'Here, Goliath. Your favourite!' Jake called, tossing an over-ripe banana towards him.

The plan worked like magic. Goliath immediately stepped out of the pool and lumbered over to the banana on the lawn. He picked it up with his trunk then shoved it into his mouth, munching it up with a look of sheer delight on his face.

'There's more,' said Jake and he and Shani quickly laid a trail of bananas all the way to where the elephants had pushed the fence down.

Seeing Goliath ambling off, the other two quickly followed him and it wasn't long before all three were back in the bush, feasting on the rest of the bananas that Jake had tossed through the gap in the fence.

'We're going to have a fix this damaged section right now,' said Rick, trying to pull up a flattened length of wire mesh. 'Otherwise Goliath and his pals will just come back again.'

Jake and Rick ran to the workshop to fetch some tools. Brandon joined them while Hannah went in to radio Morgan to get him to come and help too.

'Shani and I will make breakfast for everyone,' Sophie offered, heading back to the house, her eyes sparkling with amusement at the morning's adventure.

In the workshop, Rick pointed to a roll of strong wire fencing in one corner, 'Help me carry that will you, Brandon?' he said, while gesturing to Jake to pick up a tool box.

Jake heaved the box off the shelf and holding it in both hands, followed Rick and Brandon outside where they heard the sound of a vehicle coming up the driveway.

'I wonder who that could be?' asked Rick, pausing in front of the door.

'Morgan?' suggested Brandon.

'No. He's already here,' said Rick. 'He has his own cottage in the staff compound.'

The vehicle was now visible. It was a red jeep. Mr Sangoma's jeep, Jake suddenly realised. In all the excitement, he hadn't given a moment's thought to the visitor he was expecting that morning.

'Well, what do you know. It's Mr Sangoma,' said Brandon as the witchdoctor parked under a tree then climbed out and came towards them.

'What's he doing here?' Risk asked tersely. What with elephants in the pool and the broken fence, it sounded as if he wasn't in the mood for a visitor.

'*Jambo! Habari?*' Mr Sangoma greeted them and, noticing the wire and tools he added, 'I am sorry to trouble you. I see you have an emergency. But it is OK. I will go by myself to fetch the King Cheetah cub.'

TWELVE

'Hold on right there,' said Rick, surprise written all over his face. 'What do you mean, you'll fetch the King Cheetah cub?'

Jake wanted the ground to open up and swallow him. He shot an urgent look at the witchdoctor, desperately hoping he wouldn't say anything about the phone call yesterday.

'Well, I heard the cub was in danger,' explained Mr Sangoma. 'So it makes sense to take him to my enclosure at Duma Mfalme.'

Rick put down his end of the wire roll. 'News travels fast in these parts,' he remarked, glancing at Jake who felt worse than ever. Rick faced the witchdoctor again. 'I'm sorry, Mr Sangoma. But it makes no sense whatsoever to take the cub there. Yes, a lion killed his siblings . . .'

Jake saw a shadow pass across the witchdoctor's face.

Rick continued. 'But that doesn't give us a licence to interfere. The cub is with his mother, and that's all the protection he needs.'

'I can give him better protection,' argued the witchdoctor and Jake wanted to say something to agree with him. But he kept quiet. He was beginning to think that maybe he'd been a bit too hotheaded this time. Maybe he shouldn't have gone behind Rick's back and called the witchdoctor. But he'd been so worried about Cheepard – and still was.

'You might well be able to offer him a safe place. But you can't give him a better life.' Rick picked up the roll of wire again. 'Look, Mr Sangoma,' he said with strained politeness. 'I can't stand here arguing with you. We have a fence to mend. The cub stays where he is and that's my last word on the subject.'

The witchdoctor's face clouded over. 'I wish, then, to see him one last time,' he said.

'I have no objection to that,' said Rick. 'And Jake can go with you after he's taken the tools to the fence.' He looked at Jake and said with understanding, 'I know how much that cub means to you.' Then, lightly, he added, 'You'd better take Frances too.'

Brandon stepped in to remind them that the cheetahs had moved from their original den. 'They could be anywhere,' he said. 'You'll need telepathy or something to find them.'

'Telepathy I don't have,' said Mr Sangoma. 'But I *can* track animals. I am certain we will find the cub and his mother before the day is over.' He spoke with such confidence that Jake realised the witchdoctor could probably come at any time to take Cheepard. And no one would even know.

A feeling of confusion bubbled up inside Jake. On the one hand, he wanted nothing more than for Cheepard to be safe. But on the other, he wasn't sure he liked the idea of the witchdoctor tracking the cheetahs in Musabi without Rick's knowledge. Especially when Jake was responsible for Mr Sangoma being here today.

It didn't take long for Mr Sangoma to pick up the cheetahs' trail near the old den. 'This way,' he said, beckoning to Jake and Frances. Shani had chosen to stay behind, saying that she couldn't face another long trek in the heat!

'You two go in front,' Frances said to Jake and Mr Sangoma. 'I'll follow and keep watch just in case something tries to sneak up on us.'

'We've been lucky so far,' Jake told her. 'We haven't had any close scrapes.'

'Really?' said Frances, glancing back at the Mopane tree.

Jake rolled his eyes. It was impossible to keep a secret in this place!

Although it was only mid-morning, puffy grey clouds were building up on the horizon. Normally these would mean a storm was on the way, but Jake knew by now not to get his hopes up. Often over the past month or so the clouds had gathered in this way then dispersed as the day wore on without letting go of a single drop of rain. It was just nature's way of giving a false alarm. And it was typical of the harsh world that Jake now found so disenchanting.

They followed the cheetahs' spoor across the plain for over an hour. Every now and then, Mr Sangoma would stop and scrutinise the ground, or examine the grass or a bush, then, deciding which way Kim and Cheepard had gone, he'd walk on again. Once, when the witchdoctor looked closely at a bent stalk of grass and abruptly changed the direction in which they'd been heading, Jake said to him, 'You really know the bush, don't you?'

Mr Sangoma nodded but said nothing.

'You probably know more than Rick,' Jake added.

'I wouldn't say that,' was Mr Sangoma's only reply.

The sun beat down, burning Jake's neck, arms and legs that were already nut brown after all the time he'd spent in the open over the past few days. Finding a rare patch of shade under a small thorn tree, the three of them stopped for a short rest.

Jake took a long drink from his bottle then poured some water over his head. The refreshing sensation of cold water running down the back of his neck made him think of Goliath and his companions at the swimming pool. He could understand their delight at finding such a big source of fresh water in the midst of the dry lands.

How much longer can the animals hold out? Jake

wondered, looking across the desert-like plain. He could see a couple of giraffes a long way off. Moving gracefully along, they seemed to glide across the ground like tall ships on the sea. Somewhat closer was a family of warthogs, digging roots out of the hard earth. And then Jake saw something else – a flick of a tail and a sweep of an outstretched paw not far away in the shade of a huge ant heap – the only other bit of shade for miles around. Jake caught his breath. Could it be Kim and Cheepard?

'Look,' he whispered to Frances and Mr Sangoma. 'Over by that ant heap.' He lifted his binoculars and as he focussed them, Cheepard's little face peered round the mound of earth.

The cub stared straight at Jake and in that moment Jake thought he saw a depth of wisdom and intelligence in the cub's soft brown eyes. A wisdom perhaps that had been passed down through the ages from one King Cheetah to the next.

There was also a look of recognition on Cheepard's face so that Jake dared to hope the cub knew who he was and didn't feel threatened. 'He's seen us,' Jake whispered to the others.

Cheepard looked at them curiously for a moment then, as if he was showing off, clambered over his mother's feet that were just visible at the side of the ant heap and started tugging at the tip of her tail with his teeth.

Kim gently kicked Cheepard away with her hind

legs and rolled over so that she lay at the side of the ant heap, in full view of Jake, Mr Sangoma and Frances. It was all the invitation the cub needed. He crouched in the grass like a miniature version of the stalking adult cheetah Jake had filmed from the back of the dirt bike. Cheepard flicked his tail from side to side then sprang forward and landed on his mother's shoulders, grabbing the back of her neck in his tiny jaws.

Kim leapt to her feet and sprinted a short distance away from her cub before flopping down and looking back at him, clearly encouraging him to have another go.

'She's letting him practise his hunting moves,' Frances pointed out in a whisper.

With lightning speed, Cheepard leaped at his mother again and the pair rolled around, sharpening their skills while toning their sprinters' muscles.

'He's growing into a most wonderful animal,' said the witchdoctor with a mixture of admiration and envy. 'My people would be so proud to care for him.'

Jake tried to imagine Cheepard in the enclosure at Duma Mfalme and now, for the first time, he felt a twinge of remorse. Despite everything, Cheepard looked so much at home on the plain. Was it right to expect the cub to trade his freedom and wild ways for certain safety? Perhaps Rick was right after all.

Cheepard deserved to stay in his natural environment.

The game continued for several more minutes then, when the cheetahs grew tired, Cheepard sat up tall next to his mother and stared at Jake again. His striking face wore a look that was both gentle and majestic.

'He looks more royal than any King I've ever seen,' whispered Jake with a smile.

'Yes. He is a true King,' agreed Mr Sangoma then added, wistfully, 'How well he would look in Buhara.'

Jake was just thinking that Mr Sangoma still hadn't given up hope of taking Cheepard when he heard a deep rumbling. It was an oddly familiar, yet at the same time, strange noise. Jake's immediate thought was that there was a lion nearby but, coming to his senses, he quickly realised what the sound was. He hadn't heard it for a very long time. No wonder it sounded strange.

'Thunder!' he exclaimed and looking across to the clouds on the far northern horizon, he saw a vertical flash of lightning.

'Oh my!' breathed Frances, her voice edged with excitement. 'Let this be for real.'

'It is,' said Mr Sangoma, a smile spreading across his face. 'It definitely is.'

'How do you know?' Jake asked, fully expecting the storm, like the clouds, to come to nothing as usual.

Mr Sangoma pointed to Cheepard. 'He has

brought an end to the drought,' he said, and his eyes danced with happiness. He reached into his pocket and took out a small silver camera.

Jake could tell at a glance that it was a digital camera, one of the latest on the market. Mr Sangoma might deal in age-old mysteries and beliefs, but he was certainly right up-to-date when it came to technology!

The witchdoctor took several photographs of Cheepard and his mother, then stood up. 'It is time to go,' he urged. 'We must hurry.'

'Yes. Before the storm comes this way,' said Frances, shouldering her rifle.

'*If* it comes this way,' said Jake sceptically.

'It will. It will,' Mr Sangoma assured him. He looked at the cheetahs who were crouching up against the ant heap. '*Kwa heri*,' he said. 'Good bye. And *asante*, little King. Thank you for looking after the Buhara people.'

Jake couldn't help feeling surprised. 'Good bye?' he said. 'You mean, you're leaving Cheepard here after all?'

'But of course,' the witchdoctor told him. 'Did you think I would steal him, when your stepfather asked to keep him here?'

'Er, no,' muttered Jake. 'It's just that . . .' He trailed off, shrugging.

'He still means everything to us, so I have taken pictures to show the tribe,' Mr Sangoma explained gently. 'But as you can see,' he pointed to a fork of lightning that seemed to split the sky in two, 'his influence is very far-reaching. Even from a distance, he can bring good fortune to the Buhara. That storm is right over our tribal lands. See the shadow over there?'

Jake nodded. It looked like a huge grey sheet stretching down from the sky.

'That is rain,' said the witchdoctor. 'Glorious, soaking, life-giving rain. And it is falling on Buhara.' He put the camera back in his pocket. 'We must go,' he said with urgency. 'Soon that rain will reach us too.'

Jake's spirits soared. 'You mean it?' he said, his mind filling with images of the stranded hippos, the thin zebras, the carcasses of animals littering the plains and *shambas*, the dry landscape and empty water holes.

'Oh, yes. The drought has been broken,' said the witchdoctor. His eyes met Jake's, piercing him in a way that made Jake feel as if the witchdoctor was seeing beyond the here and now.

'The King Cheetah has not failed us,' continued Mr Sangoma, and Jake, finding himself trapped by the witchdoctor's hypnotic stare, suddenly felt as if he was also looking into Cheepard's eyes again, with the same ancient wisdom that knew more about the African bush than he could learn in a thousand lifetimes.

Mr Sangoma looked away, breaking the spell and

releasing Jake. 'It is over,' the witchdoctor said, and without another word, he turned to follow Frances.

With Frances already quite some distance ahead of them, Jake and Mr Sangoma set off as fast as they could in the sticky heat. Jake sensed an air of expectation all around. As if from nowhere, herds of antelope and zebra had gathered on the plain; they seemed restless but excited as they stamped the ground and sniffed the air.

'They know,' said the witchdoctor. 'And soon the circle of life will begin all over. The lands will come alive again. Plants will grow, there will be new births, and everywhere there will be a great abundance.' He paused and put a hand on Jake's arm. Once again, Jake could feel a strange warmth penetrating his skin. 'There will still be death,' the witchdoctor said sombrely, and he added, 'But those left orphaned will often be fostered by others. I have seen elephants adopting babies whose mothers died, and wild dogs fostering orphaned pups. And those new parents love and care for the young as if they were their very own.'

'And chimps too,' Jake put in, remembering the XYZ community he'd met in the Luama Sanctuary in Uganda. 'I've seen adult chimps adopting babies that were taken from their mothers.'

'Indeed. So you see, the animal world is in many ways much like the human world,' Mr Sangoma said. 'We belong to the natural order. And we all need each other, for we all have our place in the world. We are all connected.'

Jake jumped involuntarily as a crack of lightning snapped the air close by. It matched the flash of sudden understanding that travelled through him at the very same time. *Rick might not be my real dad but he does care for me. A lot. And that's why he's always on at me about staying safe. It's not that he's some fuddy-duddy ogre trying to spoil my fun.* And then, with big drops of cool life-giving rain beginning to fall, and the unmistakable smell of ozone that always came at the start of the rains, Jake looked at the witchdoctor and said, 'Yes, I can see that we all have our place. And mine is here, in Musabi with my mum and dad.'

It rained solidly all that night so that by early the next morning, Musabi looked completely awash.

'The veranda's flooded,' Jake said, poking his head into his parents' bedroom. The rain was so heavy it was pouring off the roof in sheets, and a strong wind was driving it onto the veranda.

'You're making a habit of bringing us bad news at the crack of dawn,' grinned Rick, sitting up in bed.

'After the drought, you can't really say a bit of flooding's bad news,' Jake joked back. He paused then, looking down at the floor, said awkwardly, 'I'm sorry I messed up. I shouldn't have gone behind your back. And you were right about Cheepard.'

'That's OK, Jake,' said Rick. 'It's all, er . . . water

under the bridge now. Just as long as you know that you and your mum are so important to me, I'd be heartbroken if anything happened to either of you.'

Jake looked up and smiled at Rick who climbed out of bed and said, 'Come on you two.' He took Hannah's arm and pretended to drag her out of bed. 'There's work to be done, lazybones!'

With the water threatening to seep in under the door and come inside, everyone gathered on the veranda with brooms and mops to sweep it away.

'This is such fun,' laughed Shani, splashing about barefoot.

'Coming from rainy old England, I never thought I'd be so thrilled to see rain,' chuckled Hannah. She pushed a huge broom across the floor to the steps, making a wave of water tumble down to the already soggy ground below.

Rick came running in from the garden. He was even more drenched than when Goliath had sprayed him. He'd been to make sure the garages weren't being flooded out, and also to check on the swimming pool. 'The cars are fine and the pool's overflowing,' he said. 'Perhaps we should have let Goliath and his mates empty it out completely yesterday.'

'Maybe that's what they were trying to do,' laughed Jake. 'They knew the rains were coming and wanted to do us a favour.'

'Yeah, I bet,' grinned Rick.

Bina had clambered onto a chair to avoid the water. She looked very confused.

'I can't remember if she's ever even seen rain before,' said Jake, giving the tiny antelope a reassuring pat.

Sophie held her mop over the wall and tried to wring it out.

'That's no good,' Brandon pointed out. 'It'll just get wetter out there.'

Jake went to help Rick and Frances roll down the canvas awnings that were usually intended to block out the sun when it shone directly onto the veranda. Now they were needed to keep the rain out. Jake untied the sash at the end of one awning and paused to listen as a deep roar sounded above the rushing rain. 'More thunder?'

The others had heard it too. But unlike thunder, it didn't stop. And all the time, it seemed to be coming closer and growing more intense.

'That's no thunder,' said Rick. He leapt onto the low wall and looked out across Musabi.

'What is it?' Jake asked, climbing up next to him so that he could also get a better look.

'Look over there,' Rick told him, pointing to the north.

Jake scanned the horizon and saw what looked like a low dark wave appearing just above the skyline. 'What is it?' he asked as more and more of the waves rolled forward across the plain so that soon it was almost completely covered by the dark rolling mass.

'It's the wildebeest!' cried Shani with delight. 'They've come back.'

Shani was right. The great herds of wildebeest had answered the call of the wild. They had sensed the rains coming and, in their hundreds, were already thundering across Musabi, returning to their summer grazing.

'This is utterly fantastic!' breathed Sophie. She ran inside and came back with the video camera, as well as several pairs of binoculars which she passed around. Then, climbing up on the wall, and unfazed by the rain driving in at her, she started filming the thrilling event.

'You can thank me for this,' chuckled Shani as they all watched the stampeding herd spilling out over the plain and coming closer every minute.

'Why?' Jake asked her.

'Well, I did a rain dance, didn't I?' she said, pretending to look serious.

'If you can call that a dance,' Jake teased her. 'And anyway, it wasn't your jumping up and down that did it. It's Cheepard who brought the rain.'

'I'd like to believe that,' said Brandon, sounding unexpectedly serious. 'It ties in perfectly with everything we have on video. The whole conflict of climate, belief and African wildlife. It's going to be the most awesome documentary!'

Down in the valley, the river was flowing rapidly as if it had never run dry. Through his binoculars Jake could see that it had already burst its banks in several places. 'To think that just yesterday, we were walking across the rocks down there,' he marvelled. He thought of Cheepard and wondered what he and Kim were doing right now. Had they found shelter, and were they as excited about the rain as the other animals?

'Mmm. Try walking across those rocks now and you'd be swept away,' said Hannah, who was standing on the wall on the other side of Rick. 'But *they* won't be,' she said, pointing down to the valley.

Jake looked to see what Hannah was talking about and saw three elephants standing next to the river, their trunks tilted up to catch the rain. 'It looks like they're worshipping the storm clouds,' Jake laughed.

'They probably are,' said Rick. 'Water is everything to elephants.'

'And not just to them. Hippos too,' said Jake, noticing a lumbering trail of river horses heading upriver along the shore. There were four of them. 'Hey! That's the herd we moved the other day!' he exclaimed. 'They must be going home.'

Sophie and Brandon were thrilled. 'I can hardly believe this,' Sophie said. 'We've got everything now.'

Brandon picked up the thread of what Sophie was saying. 'Beyond all our expectations, we have unique cheetah footage and, on top of that, we've captured drought, floods, life and death and new beginnings. And now we end where we began, with the hippos.'

Rick put his arms around Jake and Hannah's waists and drew them closer to him. 'That's Musabi for you,' he said with pride in his voice.

Down near the river, the mother hippo was carefully steering her baby along the slippery bank as if she was worried he'd fall into the swirling water.

'Isn't Musabi a great place?' Rick said to Jake.

Jake craned his neck to look up at his stepdad. 'You bet,' he said, the grin on his face matching Tambarare Duma for wideness. 'It's the best!'

This series is dedicated to Virginia McKenna and Bill Travers, founders of the Born Free Foundation, and to George and Joy Adamson, who inspired them and so many others to love and respect wild animals. If you would like to find out more about the work of the Born Free Foundation, please visit their website, www.bornfree.org.uk, or call 01403 240170.

INSTINCT
Safari Summer 5

Lucy Daniels

Living on a game reserve brings Jake Berman face to face with animals in the wild. It's exciting – and dangerous – but Jake's always ready for adventure ...

Jake is thrilled when a brand new wilderness trail opens at Musabi. It's a great chance to see the group of rare black rhinos that has just been relocated to the reserve! But when one of the rhinos is killed by poachers in pursuit of its valuable horn, the other rhinos become restless and hostile. Visitors are under threat and the whole reserve is faced with closure. Jake is convinced the poachers will come back for the rest of the rhinos. Can he persuade his stepdad to set up a stake-out, and catch them red-handed?